Good wishes

John

THE FLARE
PARACHUTE

By the same author

A Light in the Darkness, The Book Guild, 2004

THE FLARE PARACHUTE

*Based on the childhood memories of John Kidd
in the Cinq Port of Hythe, Kent
in the years 1940 to 1945*

John Kidd

Book Guild Publishing
Sussex, England

First published in Great Britain in 2007 by
The Book Guild Ltd
Pavilion View
19 New Road
Brighton, East Sussex
BN1 1UF

Copyright © John Kidd 2007

The right of John Kidd to be identified as the author of this
work has been asserted by him in accordance with the
Copyright, Designs and Patents Act 1988.

All rights reserved. No part of this publication may be
reproduced, transmitted, or stored in a retrieval system, in any
form or by any means, without permission in writing from the
publisher, nor be otherwise circulated in any form of binding
or cover other than that in which it is published and without a
similar condition being imposed on the subsequent purchaser.

All characters in this publication are fictitious and any resemblance
to real people, alive or dead, is purely coincidental.

Typesetting in Baskerville by
Keyboard Services, Luton, Bedfordshire

Printed in Great Britain by
CPI Antony Rowe

A catalogue record for this book is available from
The British Library

ISBN 978 1 84624 102 4

Remembering the men of the Royal Air Force and the United States Army Airforce who did not return.

*For our granddaughters
Charlotte Catherine
Isabelle Laura*

To my best friend

With grateful thanks to Pat Ellis and Norah Lees for their help and encouragement

1

The wind was blowing from the southwest, a sure sign of rain, thought James King as he sat down on the wooden seat that was firmly screwed to the promenade.

He looked up at the sky. Clouds had now gathered down channel and it would not stay fine for long, he knew the signs having spent his early life in the area.

From time to time white flecks appeared on the waves as they were whipped up by the blustery wind. Turning his head he could see the backs of his wife, son and daughter-in-law as they walked down the promenade in the direction of Seabrook. He had declined to do so preferring to sit on his own and gaze at the sea, lapsing into his thoughts.

The times he had been on the beach at which he was now gazing as a boy were innumerable and yet as he looked at the familiar breakwater it seemed as if it were only yesterday.

He was now looking in the opposite direction to the one his family had taken. Across the bay the outline of Dungeness nuclear power station could be seen. As a boy he would have been able to see the old lifeboat station and fishing boats hauled up on the shingle but alas both had long since gone, he thought regretfully.

A Martello tower nearby had been made into a delightful home. He could remember it during the war, when it housed two machine-guns and eight men until the danger of invasion by Hitler's army had receded. Then it was taken over by the Airsea Rescue Service. In those days coils of barbed wire ran parallel to the beach, much of it only visible at low tide.

Further up the beach anti-tank obstructions had been erected in the form of scaffold poles bolted together, whether they would have been any use was fortunately never found out.

The sound of seagulls screeching above his head caused him to look up, the wind was freshening and he dug his hands further into his pockets.

A young woman walked past accompanied by a boy of about ten or eleven years, who was carrying a smart fishing rod. It caused him to smile ruefully. He had a bamboo cane to fish with when he was his age, heavy thread for a line and a cork from a bottle with a matchstick through it as a float. They stopped; the boy had dropped the expensive fishing basket he was carrying.

'It's heavy,' he complained petulantly.

James smiled. He would have given his right arm as a boy to have had all that fishing tackle, but was the lad any happier with all that equipment? he wondered.

'Going fishing?' he smiled.

The boy looked at him arrogantly before he replied, 'No, I'm going hang gliding.'

His mother half smiled. 'Paul, really,' she chided. 'These boys,' said the woman looking at James.

'I'm sure that there is nothing wrong that the cane could not put right,' smiled James.

The woman's face suddenly lost its smile. James sniffed scornfully and looked away. Modern youth he mused, no wonder there was so much mugging.

He thought of his mother who had died some years previously and imagined her reaction if he had spoken like that; a clout on the ear from her formidable right hand would have been her first reaction.

The woman was now walking towards Stade Street which

led from the seafront to the centre of Hythe, followed by the boy who was still complaining about the weight of his equipment. She turned and observed James watching them, giving him a half apologetic smile.

He grinned. The woman had a trim figure unlike his mother who seemed to have been overweight for all of his life. Yes there was no doubt about it, people were more weight conscious these days and healthier for it.

'Expect he is going to fish in the canal,' he murmured to himself. 'Used to be full of fish years ago.'

The Royal Military canal ran right through the centre of Hythe, built in Napoleonic times to ferry troops up and down the marshes when another invasion of England was expected. As a boy James recalled it was full of roach, rudd, bream, perch, carp and the home of some massive eels. He used to sell his catch for cat food to pay for his lost hooks, in those days fish was scarce and expensive and his number twelve hooks on catgut were four pence each; a week's pocket money to him.

The hours he spent fishing; on reflection it was amazing he had never fallen in the canal.

His Great Aunt Alice had been the licensee of the North Star Inn which was situated halfway down Stade Street. When his mother's house had been hit by an incendiary bomb they had moved in with Great Aunt Alice and her companion who he had called Uncle Frank.

His own father had been called up and was serving in the Navy. It was made clear that though his mother was welcome she had to serve behind the bar, whilst he was regarded as something akin to a nuisance, hence the fact that on every opportunity summer or winter he went fishing.

In those days there were no water bailiff patrolling the canal which in any case had coils of barbed wire along each bank. This had never caused the Germans any inconvenience though it had certainly played havoc with small boys' clothing and fishing lines when they were trying to fish.

In the distance he could see a small boy throwing stones into the sea. He was wearing a school blazer which reminded him of his school in Hythe, Saint Thomas Church of England School in Saint Thomas Road which ran parallel to Stade Street. He closed his eyes; it seemed only yesterday that he was in the classroom that overlooked the green open space in the centre of Hythe.

2

Hythe, 1941

Clarence Bristol strode into the cold classroom, a little man his thinning dark hair brushed back off his forehead and kept in place with hair cream. He peered at his class through horn-rimmed spectacles as if they were unpleasant objects which to Clarence Bristol they might well have been.

His desk on its long legs was reminiscent of the type used in a city counting house in the last century, his stool also had long legs which meant that when he sat down he was able to see all the class without difficulty.

'You boy, shut the door,' snapped Mr Bristol as he lifted the lid of his desk.

A boy in a front row desk hurriedly left his seat to close the classroom door then darted back to his desk.

Clarence Bristol took the register from his desk and methodically opened it. He looked over his glasses as the class sat in an awed silence. A whisper from the back of the class caught his attention.

'Crabb, was that you?' he snapped.

'No, sir,' came the instant reply.

'Stand up boy when you speak to me.'

There was shuffling of feet and a well-made boy of about thirteen stood up.

Johnny Crabb had fair curly hair and blue eyes, his face was covered with freckles and his clothes, though clean, were well worn. He did not have a tie and his grey shirt was buttoned up at the neck with a large black button. He had two younger sisters and his father was a private with a local regiment serving out in Burma. Something of a hero to the other boys in the school, he had received the cane more than any other boy and had never been known to cry.

'If you speak again Crabb, I will cane you,' hissed Mr Bristol.

'Yes, sir,' replied Crabb, standing with a shuffling of feet.

'Sit down.'

'Yes, sir.'

Clarence Bristol began to read the register.

'Arthur,' he snapped.

'Yes, sir.'

'Barnstable.'

'Yes, sir.'

'Crabb.'

There was no reply.

'Crabb,' shouted Clarence Bristol.

'I'm here, sir,' replied a grinning Crabb.

By this time Clarence Bristol was breathing hard.

'Davies.'

'Yes, sir,' murmured a pretty dark haired girl in the second row.

'Speak up girl.'

'Yes, sir,' stuttered Julia Davies fearfully.

'Edwards.'

'Yes, sir.'

'Graham.'

'Yes, sir.'

'Johnson.'

'Yes, sir.'

'Kelly.'

'Yes, sir.'

'King.'

'Yes, sir.'

Clarence Bristol at last completed the register and then returned it to his desk; he looked up.

'Tables, nines.'

The whole class began to chant, 'Once nine is nine, two nines are eighteen, three nines are twenty seven.'

Johnny Crabb pulled at the hair of a girl sitting in front of him, she made a face and exclaimed 'Ow!'

'Six nines are fifty four,' chorused the class, 'seven nines are sixty three.'

'Stop!' bawled Clarence Bristol. A silence fell on the class.

'Crabb, stand up.'

Johnny Crabb shuffled his feet and stood up.

'Five nines Crabb?' snapped Clarence Bristol.

'Er,' mumbled Johnny.

'What was that?'

'Forty two, sir,' volunteered Johnny.

'What!' roared Clarence.

'Forty five,' whispered his pal Jimmy King.

Clarence Bristol's sharp ears heard him.

'King.'

'Yes, sir,' said Jimmy King, standing up.

'Did you speak?'

'No, sir,' replied Jimmy quickly.

'Forty five sir,' said Johnny Crabb hoping to divert attention from his pal.

'Pullen,' snapped Clarence Bristol.

The girl whose hair Johnny Crabb had just pulled stood up.

'Yes, sir,' she murmured almost in tears.

'Did King say forty five?'

'Yes, sir,' she replied fearfully.

'Come out here King,' said Clarence, his voice rising.

Jimmy King reluctantly left his desk as Clarence Bristol strode over to his cupboard and from the top shelf he took out one of his canes.

Walking slowly to the front of the class Jimmy noticed that Mr Bristol was still wearing his bicycle clips, in fact Jimmy could not ever remember him taking them off.

'Hold out your hand boy,' said Clarence as he raised the cane.

Jimmy held out his right hand, swish whack, the cane stung.

'And the other,' snapped Clarence.

Whack, whack, whack, his left hand now felt numb as well.

'Go back to your desk.'

Slowly he returned to his desk at the back of the class his hands under his armpits. Fortunately the cane had not fallen on the base of his thumbs, this was the most painful spot; one's hands ached for days and even holding a pen or pencil was painful.

Mavis Pullen flushed as Jimmy passed her desk. As Clarence Bristol returned the cane to his cupboard Johnny Crabb whispered in her ear.

'We'll get you after school, Pudden.'

Mavis Pullen ignored him, her face a brighter shade of pink.

'I'll take your knickers off and throw them in the canal.'

'You wouldn't dare,' Mavis turned around in her desk her face now bright red. 'I'll tell my mum,' she hissed.

Clarence Bristol had closed the cupboard door and turned around quickly. 'Are you talking, Pullen?' he rapped.

Mavis Pullen stood up, her face even redder.

'Sir, I –' she stuttered.

'Sit down. If you talk again I shall cane you.'

'Yes, sir,' gasped Mavis.

An ancient upright piano stood next to the cupboard

and Clarence moved towards it and then looked at the class.

'Stand, All things bright and beautiful,' he said as he stabbed a bony finger at the keyboard.

This was the limit of his musical ability as the note rang out. 'All,' he croaked, looking around the class.

'All,' sang out the class, well versed in the tuning up process of Clarence Bristol.

'Begin,' he rapped out.

'All things bright and beautiful all creatures great and small,' sang the class.

At the end of each line could be heard a sound akin to a grunt; this was not undetected by Clarence who cocked his ear and glared at the class.

'He made their glowing colours he made their tiny wings ugh ugh,' sang the class even louder.

In two strides Clarence was at his cupboard and the cane in his hand. Then he almost bounded to his desk and he brought the cane down on the lid with a sound just like a rifle shot.

'Stop!' he bawled.

The singing stopped immediately.

'Who is making that noise?'

There was no reply from the class.

'You, Kelly?'

'No, sir,' said a dark, curly-haired boy standing up.

'You, King?'

'No, sir,' replied Jimmy.

'Crabb,' he roared, 'it was you.'

'No, it wern't, sir.'

'Don't lie to me, boy.'

'I'm not sir, it were Pudden, she was farting.'

'What!' shouted Clarence Bristol.

'Yes sir, at the end of each line,' continued Johnny, his face a picture of innocence.

'I wasn't, sir,' a red-faced Mavis Pullen cut in. 'It was Crabb sir, he was making a noise like a pig at the end of each line,' said Mavis.

'Come out here, Crabb,' snarled Clarence, white-faced with anger.

'Me sir, I've done nothin',' replied Johnny, making no effort to leave his desk.

'Come out here!' yelled Clarence.

Still Johnny Crabb did not move. Clarence Bristol bounded forward between the desks and made a grab at Crabb's ear.

'Ow!' moaned Johnny as he was hauled to the front of the class.

'Hold out your hand boy,' roared Clarence, who had to let go of Johnny Crabb's ear to transfer his grip to his right wrist.

Whack, whack, whack, the cane rained down on Johnny's right hand. Clarence Bristol released it and took hold of his left wrist. Whack, whack, whack, whack, whack, suddenly he stopped.

'Now go to your desk, boy,' he said, pushing the red-faced Johnny away from him.

Johnny Crabb, his hands under his armpits, staggered back to his desk, the other boys looked at Johnny out of the corner of their eyes. Old Clarence had laid it on, but he had not cried or made a sound, which was a point of honour among them.

As the cane was returned to the cupboard Johnny Crabb leaned forward in his desk and hissed into Mavis Pullen's ear, 'I'm going to take your knickers off Pullen.'

'You do and I'll tell my dad when he comes home from the army,' whispered Mavis, half turning in her desk a triumphant note in her voice.

'You do,' replied Johnny his face almost touching the lid of his desk in an attempt to avoid Clarence Bristol's attention, 'and I'll tell him your ma's never got her knickers on either.'

'Ooh you,' replied Mavis, her face red.

Mr Bristol had returned to his desk, and looked balefully over the tops of his glasses.

'Sit,' he snapped.

There was a shuffling of feet as the class sat down at their desks their eyes on Clarence Bristol.

'Now listen all of you, I've had a complaint from a Mr Smithers in Twiss Road. A member of the Town Council.'

Since Clarence Bristol was a special constable the inspector at the Hythe Police station referred all complaints concerning youngsters to him, with some relief it should be added.

'A stone has been thrown through his greenhouse and three boys were seen running off in the direction of Stade Street. He is coming to the school to identify the boys this morning.'

'Aw Christ!' mumbled Johnny.

'Did you speak Crabb?'

'No, sir,' he replied.

'No, sir,' mimicked Clarence Bristol, 'and I suppose you know nothing about this little incident?' he said sarcastically.

'No, sir,' replied Johnny.

'Well we'll find out shortly,' said Clarence grimly. 'Get out your arithmetic books.'

There was a clatter of desk lids and the class proceeded with its arithmetic.

At ten minutes to eleven there was a tap on the door and Mr Alton the headmaster entered, as Clarence Bristol alighted from his desk stool he hastily removed his bicycle clips.

'Ah, Mr Bristol,' said the headmaster, 'I have Mr Smithers in the corridor, he has seen the other classes, can you spare a few moments?'

'Certainly, headmaster,' nodded Clarence Bristol.

The headmaster sidled up to him and muttered into his ear, 'Mr Smithers is to be one of the new Aldermen so I hear.'

'Yes, headmaster,' nodded Clarence.

'I will bring in Mr Smithers,' said Mr Alton as he left the classroom.

'Stand up, class,' snapped Clarence.

The headmaster returned with an apologetic looking individual who was obviously uncomfortable.

'Mr Smithers, Mr Bristol,' said the headmaster introducing them.

'How do you do, sir?' smiled Clarence much to the surprise of the boys who had never seen him smile before.

'I'm sorry to put you to any inconvenience Mr Bristol,' said Mr Smithers quietly.

'Not at all Mr Smithers, only too pleased to be of assistance. Look at the class and tell me if you see them. Are they on the front row sir?'

'No, Mr Bristol.'

'Sit down front row,' said Clarence.

'Next row Mr Smithers?'

'Er, no,' muttered Mr Smithers.

'Sit down second row.'

This proceeded until only the back row were standing.

'That's them, they are the boys,' said Mr Smithers, pointing at Johnny Crabb, Jimmy King and Terry Kelly.

'Those three are the culprits on the left hand side of the back row?' asked Clarence Bristol with a leer.

'Yes Mr Bristol, those three, there is no doubt in my mind,' said Mr Smithers quietly but firmly.

'Or mine Mr Smithers. Crabb, King, and Kelly, who would have thought it?' said Clarence sarcastically, turning to the headmaster.

'Who indeed,' replied Mr Alton, his lips compressed into a thin line.

'I think I can leave you to deal with the situation Mr Bristol. I've an appointment with one of the school governors, please excuse me.'

'Rest assured I will headmaster,' said Clarence as Mr Alton made to leave the classroom. Mr Smithers was about to follow him as Clarence Bristol spoke, 'Please stay Mr Smithers, I'm sure this will give you some satisfaction.' Clarence opened his cupboard door and took out his cane. The Headmaster had now departed leaving a forlorn Mr Smithers standing near the door.

'Crabb, King, Kelly, out to the front,' barked Clarence.

The three culprits ambled slowly between the desks then stood in front of the class.

'You first King, hold out your hand.'

Jimmy King held out his right hand, whack, whack whack.

'Now the left,' whack whack whack.

Jimmy struggled to keep back the tears, his hands were still numb from the earlier caning and now his right thumb had been struck by the cane. He kept blinking to keep back the tears.

'Kelly, you next,' snapped Clarence.

The cane descended and Terry Kelly was systematically dealt with.

'Now you Crabb,' said Clarence with undisguised relish.

Johnny Crabb held out his hand, Clarence Bristol had his back to Mr Smithers and could not see Johnny's face as he wielded the cane, or the fact that Johnny stuck out his tongue at Mr Smithers every time the cane fell.

When he had finished caning Crabb, Clarence Bristol turned to Mr Smithers and raised his eyebrows.

''Er, thank you Mr Bristol,' said a somewhat shaken Mr Smithers.

'Not at all Mr Smithers, I hope these boys give you no more trouble, if they do, inform me,' he said sternly.

'I will, thank you Mr Bristol,' said Mr Smithers as he hastily left the classroom.

Later in the morning when Clarence Bristol's attention was elsewhere, Johnny Crabb said to Jimmy King, 'I'm goin ter the army ranges after school dinner, yer comin?'

Jimmy nodded, 'I'll come.'

'You, Kelly?'

Terry Kelly nodded. 'Yer I'll come, might find a flare parachute over there.'

'Nar,' Johnny Crabb shook his head. 'Didn't see any come down that way last night, saw two over the golf course way, too far ter go this morning.'

A flare parachute was like a miniature of a full-size parachute and was the most prized item to be found by the boys. Pieces of shrapnel, ammunition, shell cases, even parts of enemy aeroplanes were of no comparison to a flare parachute. They were prized above any other find by the boys who had trudged miles looking for them without success.

'After dinner you will all assemble outside the caretakers store,' said Clarence Bristol, looking over his glasses. The class knew what that implied: an afternoon on the school allotments.

'And if there is any fooling about down there those concerned will receive condign punishment.' He glared at Crabb as he spoke.

'Are you listening Crabb?'

'Yes, sir,' replied Johnny.

At that moment the school bell sounded.

'Those on first dinners to the dining room; those on second into the playground; those going home go quietly,' said Clarence, putting on his bicycle clips.

The Army ranges were out of bounds to the public and

boys in particular. They were used by the School of Musketry or Small Arms School as it was called and were situated about half a mile from the school. The ranges occupied a section of shingle which stretched from the seashore to the edge of the Hythe–Dymchurch road. Rows of targets could be seen in front of mounds of earth and shingle, the targets to the seaward end of the range in order to eliminate any mishaps and when occupied red flags were hoisted on poles to give due warning.

From the school side a barbed-wire fence had been erected but this did not deter Johnny Crabb and his friends. Unknown to the army it was a regular haunt of most of the boys and the amount of ammunition collected would have kept a quartermaster occupied for some time.

Jimmy King sat quietly in his usual place in the school dining room, Johnny Crabb and Terry Kelly on either side of him. His thumbs ached and he kept rubbing them from time to time.

'Catch yer thumbs did he?' asked Johnny Crabb sympathetically. Jimmy nodded as he picked up his knife and fork and began to eat.

'I'll get the bastard one day, you see if I don't,' breathed Johnny Crabb venomously.

'It's that bloody cow Pudden's fault,' growled Terry Kelly, glaring at a table opposite them where Mavis Pullen was sitting with her friends.

'Yer,' agreed Johnny, 'I'll get 'er too,' he said as he balanced a hard lump of potato on his spoon and aimed it at the girl's table. With a flick of the wrist it sped with unerring accuracy at them and hit Mavis Pullen in the back of the neck.

'Ow,' she exclaimed, turning around.

'Stop throwing food about, Crabb,' she said in a loud voice.

Miss Darrowfield, a severe looking woman in her mid-forties and duty teacher looked across the hall.

'What's happening there?' she demanded.

'It's Crabb Miss, he is throwing food about,' spluttered Mavis.

'Come here at once Crabb,' snapped Miss Darrowfield.

Johnny left his seat and ambled over to Miss Darrowfield. He was three inches taller than she and it gave him some sort of advantage as she looked at him severely.

'Yes, Miss.'

'If you misbehave again I'll report you to Mr Bristol.'

'Yes, Miss.'

'Now return to your seat.'

'Yes, Miss.'

Miss Darrowfield watched him carefully as he resumed his place. By this time pudding had been served and it was tapioca pudding with a blob of jam placed in the centre of it. Johnny Crabb looked at his plate in disgust.

'Urg,' he said, poking at the white jelly-like mass with his spoon.

'It looks like snot,' he said, in a voice loud enough for the girls to hear.

'He's disgusting,' said Mavis, looking round at Johnny.

Unfortunately for Mavis it was at an inopportune moment as Johnny Crabb had put some on his spoon and flicked it at her and it struck the unfortunate Mavis in the eye to the delight of Terry Kelly and Jimmy King.

'Ow,' howled Mavis.

'Right in the eye, ha ha ha,' chorused Terry and Jimmy.

Mavis was now crying and trying to remove tapioca pudding from her eye at the same time.

Miss Darrowfield, attracted by the commotion, strode across the hall though the older boys like Crabb and Kelly she kept at a distance, they were beyond the school age and should have been transferred to a senior school but none was available locally. In 1941 the county authorities had far more important matters to contend with when the country was fighting for its existence than to concern themselves with the fact that there were over-age boys in the school.

'Crabb I shall report you to Mr Bristol,' she said severely.

'Why miss, I aint done nothing,' protested Johnny.

'You have not done anything Crabb,' she admonished in a vain attempt to improve his English.

'I know, thats wot I just said,' agreed Johnny, an innocent look on his face.

Miss Darrowfield realised the futility of trying to improve his English and any further discussion would be a waste of her breath. She turned on her heals and with a glare at the girls' table returned to her own meal in a more secluded part of the hall.

Having left the dining hall the boys made their way to the army range. As they trudged across the shingle Jimmy King spoke, 'Do yer think ole Barrer will tell ole Bristol?'

'Dunno,' sniffed Johnny Crabb, 'Makes no difference, he'll cane me, the ole bastard, but I'll get im one day, you see if I don't,' Johnny's face screwed up with hatred.

Jimmy King and Terry Kelly exchanged glances.

'Ow yer goin ter do that?' asked Terry.

'I will, I will,' muttered Johnny through his teeth.

They crawled under the barbed-wire fence each holding the wire up for the other, then they spread out and for the next twenty minutes scoured the dunes and shingle foreshore.

Jimmy King shouted and pointed. 'The red flag's going up.' Johnny Crabb ran towards him turning to Terry Kelly behind him.

'Come on Kelly, we'd better get back.'

They both joined Jimmy and they began to trudge back the way they had come.

'Anyway we done alright,' said Johnny, taking some clips of live .303 ammunition from his pocket.

''Ow many clips did you get Kingsy?'

'Four clips,' replied Jimmy.

'You, Kelly?'

'Three,' replied Terry.

'I got five,' said Johnny who suddenly stopped and pointed to something in a clump of grass.

''Ere, look,' he said bending down.

'A grenade,' as he was about to pick it up Terry Kelly spoke.

'Is it safe? Don't look like there's any pin in it.'

'It 'ud gorn off if it wasn't safe wouldn't it?' said Johnny, picking up the grenade.

'S'pose so,' agreed Jimmy, 'what are you goin ter do wiv it?'

Johnny Crabb shrugged. 'Clokey might swop it for his flare parachute,' he replied.

Jimmy King made a face and shook his head doubtfully. 'Don't fink so, I've offered all my shrapnel, all my ammunition, my aunt's gas mask and a bit of that German plane that crashed over the back of barrack hill.'

Terry Kelly nodded his agreement as he sniffed, 'And I offered him a bit of that Messerschmitt, two shell cases, all my shrapnel and ammunition, my gran's gas mask and our cat, but he wouldn't.'

'I'll find something ter do with it,' said Johnny, putting the grenade into his pocket.

'Couldn't we make a parachute?' said Terry suddenly.

'Where we gonna get silk from eh?' said Johnny impatiently.

'My mum's got some silk bloomers, my dad brought them home when he was last on leave.'

Johnny Crabb stopped walking and turned to Terry Kelly.

'Yer, thats a good idea, can yer get 'em, we could try,' said Johnny hopefully.

'Nar, she'd find out,' said Terry, having second thoughts on the matter.

'Why?' said Jimmy quickly.

'My brother Peter, that's why,' said Terry.

Peter Kelly was some three years younger than his elder brother.

'He'd tell her,' said Terry miserably.

'You tell 'im I'll bash 'im if he does,' said Johnny aggressively.

'You won't,' said Terry quietly. Though he considered his younger brother a pest at times there was a protective streak in Terry and he would not let any of the older boys bully him.

'I'll get 'em,' said Terry, his jaw set.

'When can you get them?' asked Jimmy.

'Dunno, I'll try,' replied Terry.

'Allotments this afternoon,' said Jimmy picking up a stone and hurling it at a seagull that had flown near them.

'Better'n class,' said Johnny, looking at the grenade again.

'We could pelt Clokey and his gang if their class is down there,' suggested Terry.

'They won't be after last time, old Alton said only one class at a time,' said Jimmy miserably.

'Nar,' agreed Johnny, pushing the grenade back into his pocket. 'What did old Bristol mean by condign punishment?'

'Dunno,' remarked Terry.

'I think it means he canes yer bum instead of yer 'ands,' said Jimmy reflectively.

'Does he, the ole shit,' said Johnny grinding his teeth. 'I'll get 'im one day you see,' he sniffed.

The boys squeezed back under the barbed-wire fence and began to run back to school. They could hear the bell in the distance and ran faster but they were still late.

The class had assembled in the playground outside the caretaker's store when they arrived back at school. Fortunately as yet Clarence Bristol had not missed them. Jimmy and Terry got at the end of the queue of their classmates waiting to be issued with a gardening implement. The procedure was always the same: girls were given a rake or hoe and boys a spade or fork, with the two biggest boys being given the two wooden wheelbarrows.

Clarence Bristol walked along the line as they waited for Mr Turner the caretaker to give them a gardening tool. He suddenly spotted Jimmy and Terry at the end of the line.

'Where's Crabb?' he rapped.

'I think he's gorn for a pee sir,' said Terry.

Clarence Bristol made a clicking noise of exasperation, 'Kelly, use the correct term boy, he has gone to the urinal.'

'Yes, sir,' replied Terry.

A that moment Johnny Crabb came ambling across the playground.

Clarence Bristol glared at him. 'Hurry up boy,' he bawled.

Johnny Crabb moved slightly faster.

'Hurry.'

Clarence Bristol stood with his hands on his hips with his bicycle clips on and with his slim build he looked something akin to a male ballet dancer as he awaited Crabb.

'I've been for a pee sir,' said Johnny when he was a pace or two from him.

Knowing full well the futility of trying to improve Crabb's grammar Clarence did not try. 'I've been informed Crabb that you were throwing food about in the dining hall,' he rasped.

'I wasn't, sir,' protested Crabb.

Clarence sprang forward and grabbed Crabb's right ear. 'Don't lie to me, boy,' he snarled as he propelled the still protesting Crabb to the front of the queue.

'Ow ow,' yelled Crabb as Clarence Bristol gripped his ear.

'A wheelbarrow and spade for Crabb if you please Mr Turner,' said Clarence, still gripping the hapless Crabb's right ear.

'Yes, Mr Bristol,' grinned the caretaker who had little love for Johnny Crabb.

Clarence Bristol at last released Crabb's now bright-red ear.

'Take that wheelbarrow Crabb and go to the front of the line where I can see you and if there is any fooling about I'll deal with you later.'

'Saucy little bleeder that one,' sniffed the caretaker as he watched Crabb push the wheelbarrow away.

Clarence Bristol chose to ignore the remark as he beckoned to Terry Kelly.

'Kelly, get the other wheelbarrow and stand next to Crabb where I can see you both.'

'Yes, sir,' said Kelly as he gripped the handles of the wheelbarrow.

Unfortunately for the caretaker Terry Kelly's judgement of distance was not good and he pushed the wheelbarrow over the caretaker's foot.

'Ow, watch out,' yelled the caretaker.

'You stupid boy,' snapped Clarence as he cuffed Kelly on the ear.

'Ow,' cried Kelly, letting go of the heavy wooden

wheelbarrow which fell on its side right on the unfortunate caretaker's other foot.

'You stupid bleeder!' howled the caretaker as he jumped backwards clutching his foot.

'Pick it up, pick it up,' roared Clarence Bristol, who was aware that Crabb was doubled up laughing at the end of the line. Much to the caretaker's relief Mr Bristol's class at last left the playground and the crocodile of reluctant gardeners led by Crabb and Kelly slowly wound its way down the road to the allotments.

The school allotments were situated adjacent to the canal, behind the Romney, Hythe and Dymchurch Light Railway station. This was a distance of some quarter of a mile and after fifty yards Clarence Bristol had cause to regret sending Terry Kelly and Johnny Crabb to the front.

The column had almost come to a halt as Clarence hastened to the head of the crocodile.

'Get a move on you two, we haven't got all day,' he snapped.

Kelly and Crabb quickened their stride and he returned to the rear of the column.

After another fifty yards the crocodile had slowed almost to a snail's pace and Clarence Bristol almost flew to the front of the almost stationary column.

'What did I tell you, Crabb?' he snarled.

'These barrers are 'eavy, sir,' replied Crabb truculently.

'Don't be impertinent boy, they are empty.'

'Our spades are in them,' retorted Johnny.

This was enough for Clarence Bristol, his hand again fastened on Johnny Crabb's ear.

'Come to the back of the column you two where I can see you better, Davies and Vincent lead on,' he said to the two boys walking behind Crabb and Kelly.

With Kelly and Crabb at the rear of the column progress improved until Crabb pushed his wheelbarrow into the legs of Mavis Pullen who had the misfortune to be walking in front of him.

Clarence Bristol did not see the incident as he was negotiating their passage across a road, holding up his arms to stop non-existent traffic.

'He keeps pushing his wheelbarrow into me,' wailed Mavis, dropping her rake in the road.

'She wants ter walk faster,' retorted Johnny Crabb.

Clarence Bristol glared at Crabb as he rejoined them on the pavement and then walked beside him.

'If you do not behave boy, I'll thrash you,' he said venomously.

Crabb did not speak, his mouth clamped tight and the muscles of his young jaw were clearly discernible.

The class finally arrived at the school allotments, and once some semblance of order and work allocation was made, Clarence would light the rubbish heap and stand with his back to it in an effort to keep warm.

Then he would direct operations like some latter-day Capability Brown whilst the class would make their doubtful efforts. For a half an hour some sort of progress was made under Clarence Bristol's gimlet gaze, and even Johnny Crabb was putting rubbish into his wheelbarrow on the far side of the allotment. Clarence watched him as he filled the wheelbarrow, then pushed it along the footpath that ran around the periphery of the allotments until he reached the spot where he was standing. 'Shall I put this rubbish on, sir?' said Johnny politely.

Clarence Bristol nodded but did not speak. Crabb pushed the wheelbarrow behind Clarence Bristol and unseen by him pushed a clip of ammunition on the heap. Quickly he emptied the wheelbarrow then beat a hasty retreat to the other side of the allotment to refill the wheelbarrow. Meanwhile the class carried on with questionable ability.

'Don't stand on those plants, you brainless oaf,' roared

Clarence as one of the less green-fingered members of the class stood on a row of young onions.

'You, girl, watch what you are doing with that hoe, have you fallen asleep King? Do something, boy.'

Mavis Pullen was on the canal bank getting some water in an old watering can to spray on the seedlings in a cold-frame when suddenly there was a loud bang.

Clarence Bristol bounded forward three feet as if on a spring, a second bang caused confusion on the allotments, then there was a splash and a yell from Johnny Crabb.

'Pudden's fallen in, sir,' he shouted from the canal bank.

Clarence Bristol, still shaken, now lost all interest in the rubbish heap and bounded across the allotments.

Mavis Pullen, though not out of her depth, was splashing about and screaming at the same time. Clarence grabbed a hoe and stretched out to Mavis.

'Grab it, girl,' he shouted.

A crowd of children now hemmed Clarence in. Johnny Crabb pushed a boy in front who fell against the back of Clarence Bristol's legs, which caused him to lose his balance and with a cry he followed Mavis into the canal. A subdued cheer arose as Johnny Crabb picked up a rake and elbowed his way to the canal bank.

Clarence Bristol was spluttering in the water, the thick mud on the bottom of the canal seemed to be sucking him down. In his panic he fell forward and almost disappeared under the water. As his head appeared Crabb rammed the rake into his ear.

'Ow, ouch,' bellowed Clarence as he lost his balance again.

'Grab it, sir,' said Johnny gleefully.

Meanwhile Mavis had struggled to the bank and was coughing violently on the grass.

Clarence, who had now lost his glasses, reappeared again

and this time he grabbed at the rake and was hauled spluttering to the bank by a grinning Johnny Crabb. Covered with mud and weed from the canal Clarence almost fell in a heap when he got out.

'You're sitting on some lettuce plants sir,' said a voice which sounded like Terry Kelly's.

When Clarence had somewhat recovered his breath, he immediately told the class to clean their gardening tools as they were returning to school.

'Where's Mavis Pullen?' he croaked.

'I'm here, sir,' wailed Mavis, whose clothes were sticking to her overweight body.

'It was Crabb's fault sir, he threw a lump of earth at me.'

'I didn't, it was yours you silly fat cow, falling in,' he retorted.

'Be quiet,' gasped Clarence, whose voice appeared to be going. 'I'll investigate this, never fear. Form up out on the pavement.'

As the column approached the school precinct Mr Alton, alerted by the noise, looked out of his office window. He frowned and looked at the clock on the wall which said 2.45. Thinking it had stopped he took out his pocket watch; his office clock was indeed correct.

'What on earth are they coming back for?' he muttered as he left his office to meet them.

Clarence Bristol had still not recovered from his immersion in the canal and his voice faltered from time to time. The headmaster met them as they entered the playground and his mouth opened in surprise as he beheld Clarence Bristol's bedraggled state.

'What has happened?' demanded Mr Alton.

'I, er, head,' choked Clarence before his voice failed.

"E fell in, sir,' announced Johnny Crabb importantly. 'Went right under sir, I pulled him out with a rake.'

'Good heavens,' gasped the headmaster.

'I, er,' gurgled Clarence.

'Go home immediately Mr Bristol, you will catch your death of cold. Go and have a hot bath,' said Mr Alton.

'He smells, too,' said a voice which was ignored.

Clarence Bristol, who was now shivering, nodded violently.

'I will take your class, you go home and get out of those wet things,' said Mr Alton as Clarence began to stagger in the direction of the staff cycle shed.

'Into your classroom after you have given your garden tools to Mr Turner,' said Mr Alton.

The class trooped off across the playground towards the caretaker's shed as the headmaster watched Clarence Bristol cycle none too happily down the road outside the school.

'Crabb,' the headmaster shouted, just as Johnny was about to give his wheelbarrow to the caretaker, who looked balefully at him. 'Crabb!' the headmaster's voice reverberated around the playground.

Johnny immediately let go of the wheelbarrow and turned to run back to the headmaster. Unfortunately the heavy wooden wheelbarrow again fell on its side and for the second time that day the caretaker did not move quickly enough. Not only did the wheelbarrow land on his other foot but the spade fell out and hit his knee. The caretaker let out a yell of anguish as he bellowed, 'You bloody stupid little bleeder,' after the departing Crabb.

The Headmaster's view of what had happened had been obscured by a crowd of children but he was not going to tolerate language like that from a member of his staff. He strode angrily across the playground to the caretaker who was still rubbing his kneecap.

'Your language, please, I'm expecting the vicar at any moment, what on earth would he think?'

'It's that little,' the caretaker paused with difficulty and pointed at Crabb.

'It weren't my fault sir, barrer's no good, look, one leg is shorter than the other.'

The headmaster looked at the wheelbarrow still lying on its side. As a gardener himself he knew that it would not balance properly.

'It needs repairing, then it won't topple over,' he said tersely. 'Come with me Crabb,' snapped Mr Alton, now in ill humour. Johnny followed him into school, down the corridor and into his office. When he had closed the door he spoke.

'Now Crabb, how did Mr Bristol fall in? I want the truth mind.'

'Well sir, Pudden fell in first,' he began.

'Pudden!' frowned Mr Alton.

'Mavis Pullen, sir,' replied Crabb.

'She did? Where is she?' The headmaster's face paled as he had not seen her in the playground.

'She's gorn 'ome, Mr Bristol told 'er.'

'Go on,' nodded the headmaster, somewhat relieved.

''E tried to get 'er out wiv a hoe but fell forward into the canal when she pulled on the hoe.'

'I see,' murmured Mr Alton.

'Then Kingy and Kelly pulled Pudden out, and I pulled 'im out wiv a rake sir,' said Johnny, obviously enjoying his newly-acquired importance.

'Hm,' the headmaster pursed his lips. It seemed too good to be true as far as Crabb, King and Kelly were concerned. 'You may go to your class Crabb. Tell them to take out their reading books and read quietly,' said Mr Alton as he stared thoughtfully out of his office window.

'Yes, sir,' replied Johnny. He left the office and closed the door with a loud bang.

Albert Alton visibly shook as the noise descended on his eardrums, and he slowly shook his head as he listened to Crabb's boots clatter down the corridor.

* * *

Johnny, blissfully unaware of the sour look now appearing on his headmaster's face, strode into the classroom.

'Get your books out and start reading,' said Johnny as he got onto Clarence Bristol's stool. He was greeted by a chorus of laughter and comments.

'You are not in charge, Crabb,' said Doreen Chambers haughtily.

'Oh yes I am, Miss Piss Pot Chambers, get your reading book out,' retorted Crabb.

'You are not, Crabb, anyway someone's coming,' retorted Doreen.

In a flash Johnny had left Clarence's stool and with a clatter rushed to his own desk, just as the classroom door opened and the headmaster appeared.

The following day Clarence Bristol, much to the relief of his class did not arrive at school. His wife came to inform Mr Alton that he had a bad chill and the doctor had said he should stay in bed for the next three days. His absence was discussed at length in the playground during playtime by members of his class.

'If 'e'd gone in at the Red Lion bridge or the Nelson bridge 'e might 'ave drowned; it's deeper there,' remarked Jimmy King.

'Yer,' agreed Terry Kelly, 'I don't fink he can swim.'

'Nar, I don't fink so neither,' sniffed Johnny Crabb.

For the next few days school was tolerable for them. Though Mr Alton would use the cane on occasions at the present time he was well disposed towards Johnny Crabb and his friends. This happy state of affairs soon came to an end and within a week Clarence Bristol was back at school, and his enforced rest had not improved his temper.

On reflection he had considered that he had been made a complete fool of by Crabb and he was going to exact just retribution. How much Mavis Pullen was responsible for this Johnny was uncertain but Pinky Johnson had seen Clarence leaving the Pullen house one evening and he had told Terry Kelly. Johnny Crabb was now receiving the cane on every possible pretext but never once had he cried or made a fuss.

Some days later Clarence arrived in class in a foul mood, brought about by one of the regular police officers asking him if he had been swimming in the canal lately. The class were all at their desks as he strode into the classroom. Taking a cane from his desk he lashed the top of his desk sending a sound like a rifle shot around the classroom.

'Tables, eights,' he snapped.

'Eight ones are eight,' intoned the class.

'Eight twos are sixteen, eight threes are twenty four.'

'Stop,' the cane crashed down on his desk again.

'Crabb, eight sevens?'

'Fifty six sir,' came the reply much to Clarence Bristol's surprise.

'Carry on.' The cane come down on the desktop again.

When the class had finished the eight times table Clarence lashed the desk top again.

'Twelves.' When the class had finished he opened his desk.

His eyes immediately fell on a hand grenade and his face went pale. Carefully he lowered the lid of the desk.

'Go and get the headmaster, Chambers,' he said to a girl in the front row.

'Yes, sir,' replied Doreen Chambers, leaving her desk.

'Who put that hand grenade in my desk?' His eyes fell on Crabb.

'You, Crabb?' The fear that was on his face took the venom out of his voice.

Mr Alton entered the classroom and looked about.

'What is it, Mr Bristol?' he asked testily.

'In my desk sir, a hand grenade,' said Clarence in barely a whisper. 'Without a pin in it.'

'What!' said the headmaster incredulously.

Mr Alton, who had been a soldier in the first World War, stepped forward and gingerly opened the desk.

Yes, there it was, a new one obviously, without its safety pin.

Gently he lowered the lid of the desk and looked at the class.

'Who put it there?' he asked grimly as he faced the class.

Johnny Crabb, well aware that he would be blamed, no matter what, put up his hand.

'I did sir, I found it out on the dunes, I put it there for safety sir as Mr Bristol is a special constable, I think it's a dud sir.'

'A dud,' gasped Mr Alton, 'how could you know that boy?'

'Sir, I,' began Johnny.

'Be silent Crabb, everyone file out to the playground quietly and stand on the class line, the other classes must be informed.'

'I will do that, headmaster,' said Clarence.

'I will telephone the army; they must remove it at once,' said the headmaster as they vacated the classroom.

3

Captain George Anderson of the Royal Army Ordnance Corps drove slowly through the centre of Hythe. He slowed down at the Grove cinema and then turned left at the Nelson public house and slowly approached the wooden pontoon bridge that spanned the canal, the original bridge having been destroyed at the beginning of the war when an invasion was thought imminent.

'Sounds like a practical joke to me, Sam,' he said to the sergeant sitting next to him, as the vehicle rattled over the bridge.

'Boys will be boys, sir,' grinned Sergeant Sam Ellison.

'Won't they just,' chuckled George Anderson.

'Still, it will give us a chance to talk to the kids about those new anti-personnel bombs.'

'Those butterfly bombs,' the sergeant's face hardened.

'Aye, that's the beasties,' said the captain.

'Bloody vicious invention, just the sort of thing that kids would pick up,' snarled the sergeant.

'Makes you wonder what we are fighting,' said the captain with almost resignation in his voice. The whole school was now assembled in the playground.

''Ere comes old Alton,' said Jimmy to Johnny Crabb.

They were at the back of the throng trying to go unnoticed. Clarence Bristol stood at the front of his class mopping his brow with a handkerchief, still a little unnerved by what had happened.

'You will all stay here,' announced the headmaster, 'until the grenade has been removed from the premises.'

'Can we go 'ome, sir?' said a voice from the back of the playground.

'No, you cannot,' said the headmaster angrily.

'Who was that boy?'

'Crabb I think, sir,' replied Clarence Bristol weakly.

'I will deal with him later,' snapped the headmaster.

The army vehicle pulled up outside the school and the captain jumped out. With a flourish he opened the playground gate and marched towards the assembled children.

'Good morning,' he began as he approached the teachers. 'Are you the headmaster?' The captain brushed his rather fine auburn moustache with the back of his fingers.

'I am,' replied Mr Alton.

'Captain Anderson,' he said, holding out his hand.

'Albert Alton,' said the headmaster as he shook hands.

The sergeant had now entered the playground with a heavy steel box with a handle on each side of it.

'My sergeant is bringing a box into which we can pop the blighter. 'Where is it, sir?'

'This way, captain,' said Mr Alton as he led the two soldiers past the staff and into the school.

Johnny Crabb and company were engaged in animated conversation, the subject being the soldiers' boots and the noise that they had made when they crossed the playground.

'Cor, wouldn't I like a pair like that,' enthused Johnny.

'Yeh, wiv all them blakeys in them,' agreed Jimmy.

'Smashing,' added Terry.

The soldiers suddenly emerged from the building carrying the box between them, followed by the headmaster. They put down the heavy steel box and straightened up.

'It's convenient headmaster, as it happens,' began the captain, 'I was going to call on you regarding an anti-personnel mine which it seems is aimed at children.'

'Really, Captain?' replied Mr Alton, raising an eyebrow.

'Yes, a type that will attract kids, mind anything attracts them what?' he nodded at the box and grinned.

'Yes,' the headmaster's lips became a thin line, 'the boy concerned with that grenade will be punished I assure you,' he snapped.

'At least the boy did not play with it in the playground for example,' said the captain. 'We have had a number of cases reported to us of kids playing with live ammunition, very nasty I can tell you,' he grimaced.

The headmaster now realised that matters had turned out rather well and perhaps Crabb should not be punished after all.

'Was it a dud mister?' said a voice from the back of the playground.

The captain turned to face the children and smiled. 'We do not know yet,' he replied amiably.

''Ow d'yer find out?' another demanded.

'We make experiments,' replied the captain.

''Ow?' came the reply.

'It's a dud I tell yer,' came the unmistakable voice of Johnny Crabb.

'I'll show you what it's all about,' said the captain, unused to the jibes of twelve- and thirteen-year-old boys. 'Just how dangerous these things are.' He indicated to the sergeant to pick up the box as he marched down the playground. A high wall at the far end marked the school boundary, the other side being open ground.

The captain disappeared through a side gate. Moments later he reappeared in the playground. Meanwhile the sergeant had placed the box at the base of the wall.

Before anyone could move or say a word the captain had opened the box, picked up the grenade and hurled it over the wall. Suddenly there was a loud explosion, and gasps from the children.

'Cor,' gasped Johnny Crabb, 'it ain't a dud.'

The headmaster looked up at the sky as if imploring divine help whilst Clarence Bristol had fainted.

The headmaster and the two soldiers carried Clarence into school, whilst a voice could be heard asking, 'Is he dead, sir?' The headmaster glared in the direction of the voice as he disappeared from view.

When they emerged again the headmaster could be heard saying, 'It was an unnecessary thing to do captain, even irresponsible if I may say so.'

'I object to that, sir,' replied the captain. 'The other side of the wall was perfectly clear, I made sure of that, and it gave the youngsters a surprise.'

'And our Mr Bristol,' remarked Mr Alton.

'Yes, quite,' smiled the captain. 'But the fact is they now know that they are dangerous, that is the point of a practical demonstration.'

'Perhaps you are right, captain,' said the headmaster, his manner more friendly.'

'I know I am, sir,' replied the captain. 'Sam, stow that box and bring me that model of the butterfly bomb.'

'Yes sir,' replied the sergeant, picking up the box. It had started to rain and the headmaster signalled to Miss Darrowfield.

'Into the assembly hall please Miss Darrowfield. First row file in quickly and quietly.'

The children hurried forward to get out of the rain.

'I said quietly, Kimber,' the headmaster glared at a stocky ten-year-old boy who seemed to be trying to stamp his feet as he walked into school.

When the school were all seated on the floor of the assembly hall and the staff on chairs at the back, joined by a now recovered Clarence Bristol, the captain began his talk. He stood on the rostrum facing the assembly and posed as if he was directing an army campaign.

'You have just seen boys and girls the power of a hand grenade.' The captain smiled in the direction of Clarence Bristol who looked far from happy. 'In the playground it could have killed all of us, remember that.' He paused for a moment.

'Now I have here, ah thank you sergeant,' he said as Sergeant Ellison handed him a brightly coloured object. He held the object up which looked like a cocoa tin with two wings attached to it. The piece that looked like a cocoa tin was painted bright yellow and the wings or arms were red with yellow spots on them. The captain smiled and looked at a pretty little girl sitting on the front row. 'Why do you think we call it a butterfly bomb my dear?'

The little girl hesitated and put a hand across her mouth. 'Come on,' coaxed the captain, 'don't be shy, tell me.'

'Because it looks like a butterfly sir,' she mumbled.

'That's right, because it looks like a butterfly, good girl,' said the captain, now getting into the swing of things. 'If you see one do *not* touch it or pick it up,' he paused, his eyes twinkling.

The headmaster was expecting a remark about not putting one in a master's desk but thankfully it did not materialise

'Its arms or wings here,' the captain moved them carefully, 'if touched cause it to go off.'

The whole school watched fascinated and in complete silence.

'Look, I'll pass it around so you can all see it,' said the captain. He stepped forward, bent down and gave it to the pretty little girl who had spoken

Johnny Crabb's hand shot up to the consternation of the headmaster and Clarence Bristol.

'Yes, laddie,' said the captain.

'Is it a dud, sir?' The captain smiled. 'It's a model son, made out of wood with two springs to show how the wings or arms work. Now pass it round and take a good look at it, do not touch it if you see one. If you do, tell your teacher or a policeman.'

As fate would have it by the time the model reached Johnny Crabb it was distinctly the worst for wear.

'Sir,' piped up Terry Kelly, 'the wings 'ave come off.'

Mr Alton and Clarence Bristol exchanged glances.

'I'll deal with you later, Kelly,' said a fully recovered Clarence Bristol.

'No harm done,' said the captain, hastily retrieving his battered model.

'I didn't do it sir, Pudden went and sat on it,' protested Terry.

'I didn't, sir,' squeaked the plump Mavis Pullen.

A broad grin appeared on the sergeant's face as the headmaster stood up.

'Will you be silent, Kelly,' he said angrily.

'Could you do another experiment with one sir, like yer did with the grenade?' asked Georgie Cloke.

'Er no, no,' replied the captain.

'Why not?' asked another voice.

The captain decided it was now prudent to take his leave and spoke quickly. 'I've some new posters headmaster, could they be pinned up?'

'Certainly captain,' came the reply.

'Good, thank you sir, I'll get some from our vehicle, then we'll be orf.'

The captain and his sergeant, accompanied by the headmaster, left the assembly hall. At the army vehicle he gave some coloured posters to the headmaster.

'Goodbye sir,' said the captain, holding out his hand and glancing at the school. 'I was beginning to wonder which of us has got the more nerve-wracking job.'

Mr Alton shook his hand and smiled thinly as he replied, 'It's marginal captain. Good luck to you both sergeant.'

The two soldiers climbed into their vehicle and drove away whilst Mr Alton retraced his steps across the school playground.

4

Terry Kelly leaned against the playground wall as he cut a pattern on a piece of wood with his clasp knife.

''Ere Crabby,' he said as he stopped cutting, 'old Ma Tennant's gotta pineapple.'

Johnny Crabb, who was wrestling with his pal Jimmy King, suddenly released his hold on Jimmy.

'A what?' he said, curiosity in his voice.

'A pineapple,' replied Terry.

'What the bleedin 'ell's that?' demanded Jimmy, his pugnacious face screwing up in disgust.

'It's a fruit, my mum says,' explained Terry.

'It's in a bowl in their front room winder.'

'Is it?' sniffed Johnny, unimpressed.

''Ave you seen one Kingy?' asked Terry.

Jimmy shook his head. 'Nar never,' he replied.

'She's got some bananas too,' continued Terry, 'and oranges, all in this bowl. Clokey and me were looking at it last night.'

'Were yer,' said Johnny with a sniff.

The bell rang for second dinner sitting and Terry folded the blade of his clasp knife.

'I'm going 'ome fer dinner terday,' Johnny said, turning to make his way out of the school playground.

'Me mum's got some mackerel and they won't keep til ternight,' explained Johnny as he bounded to the playground gate, leaving Terry and Jimmy to file into school with the rest of the pupils on the second dinner sitting.

'I'm goin ter see it again,' said Terry as he spooned a

large portion of potato into his mouth.

'When?' said Jimmy, poking at his boiled potato.

'Ternight.'

'These taters are burnt yer know,' said Jimmy looking at Terry with some distaste.

'Are they?' frowned Terry.

'Bloody are,' said Jimmy pushing his plate away in disgust.

'Taste alright ter me,' replied Terry, piling up his spoon again.

'Crabby's right yer know,' said Jimmy, his nose wrinkling.

'Oh,' mumbled Terry his mouth full again.

'You'd eat 'orse shit if it 'ad batter round it,' said Jimmy with some feeling.

At that moment Clarence Bristol, who was the duty teacher, walked past their table. He stopped and looked at them.

'And what is wrong with your dinner King?' he demanded, his hands on his hips. Most of the school would have greeted his question with abject silence, such was his menacing attitude, not so Jimmy.

'The potaters are burnt sir,' he said in a loud voice. There was a hush in the dining hall and Miss Darrowfield, who had formed the same opinion, put a hand across her mouth as she sat at the staff dining table.

The cook, who was a relative of Clarence Bristol and a law unto herself, was not a person to accept complaints or criticism in any form from anyone, least of all the pupils.

'Burnt,' repeated Clarence, his voice rising.

'Yes, sir,' said Jimmy with feeling.

'There are plenty of boys and girls in this world King who would be glad to have those potatoes,' snapped Clarence. 'Do you know that boy?' he added, his patience ebbing.

'No, sir, replied Jimmy at last.

'Let me inform you there are,' said Clarence, sourly convinced that he had made his point.

'Then they can 'ave mine sir,' said Jimmy, pushing his plate away.

Clarence Bristol took a deep breath and strode behind Jimmy's chair. His hand shot out and long fingers grabbed his right ear. 'Are you being impertinent boy?' he growled, twisting Jimmy's ear.

'Ow, ow, no, sir,' cried Jimmy his head now on one side.

'You will eat every scrap of your dinner before you leave this table,' hissed Clarence, giving his ear a final twist before releasing it.

Jimmy gingerly touched his now bright red right ear before resuming his dinner. It did not help to know that Mavis Pullen and her friends on the opposite table were smiling and giggling at his expense.

Some minutes later when puddings were being served Jimmy picked his boiled potato from his plate and leaned under the table. With a gentle flick of his wrist he tossed it under the girls' table unbeknown to all save a grinning Terry Kelly, who was now attacking his sponge pudding.

By the time the meal was concluded Mavis and the other occupants of her table had trodden the potato into the polished wood block floor and as they were about to leave the eagle-eyed Clarence spotted the mess.

'What is all this mess?' he bellowed.

The girls were stunned into silence. Jimmy and Terry were about to leave and suddenly attracted his attention.

'King come here,' he roared.

'Yes, sir,' said Jimmy coming forward.

'Where's your dinner?'

'I 'anded it in, sir,' replied Jimmy.

'And I did not see it,' fumed Clarence.

'It was clean, sir,' protested Jimmy.
'Ask Miss Darrowfield, she saw me.'

At the sound of her name Eileen Darrowfield walked towards them.

'I did see him Mr Bristol,' she said quickly, 'his plate was clean.'

'Thank you, Miss Darrowfield,' he replied. 'You may go, King,' he snapped.

Jimmy flashed Miss Darrowfield a look of thanks and hurried out of the hall but not before he heard Mr Bristol give a detention for all the mess under the table.

'And you can clear it up,' said Clarence angrily. 'Get a cloth Chambers, hurry girl.'

'Yes, sir,' stuttered Doreen Chambers as she rushed towards the kitchen

'Look at your shoes!' Miss Darrowfield pointed to the marks the soles of her shoes were making on the polished wood block floor; white marks were appearing everywhere. 'Take your shoes off Chambers and clean them,' said Miss Darrowfield her voice rising.

'What a mess,' observed Mrs Woolett, the infant teacher, as she passed by them.

By this time Mr Turner, the school caretaker, had arrived on the scene as he was responsible for polishing the floor.

'Gawd's strewth what a—' he began.

'It's being cleaned up, Mr Turner,' said Clarence tersely, 'and the culprits punished.'

This mollified the lazy, short-tempered caretaker who, swiftly departed from the scene to the relative peace of his shed.

The Tennants' pineapple was still the subject of the boys' conversation during afternoon lessons.

'It looks like a shrunken 'ead,' said Terry Kelly when Clarence Bristol had his back to the class.

'I am going ter see it after school,' said Jimmy King.

'My mum says ole Ma Tennant is a bleeding show off,' retorted Johnny Crabb.

'Are you talking, Crabb?' rapped Clarence as he rounded to face the class.

'No, sir,' replied Johnny standing up at his desk with the maximum of noise.

'If you talk again I will cane you, sit down,' said Clarence, looking over the top of his glasses.

'Yes, sir,' replied Johnny, sitting down and managing to bang his desk lid as he did so.

Clarence glared at him and then took out his Bible in an effort to try and impart some religious knowledge to the class. He began to read the parable of Jesus Christ turning water into wine at a wedding he was attending. This evoked some interest from Jimmy King who, with his elbows on his desk and chin cupped in his hands, listened with rapt attention. His unusual attitude caught Clarence Bristol's eye and he was unwise enough to try and find out what was passing through one of his more errant pupil's mind.

'And have you any questions to ask about this miracle King?' he asked, his manner unusually benign.

'Yes, sir,' said Jimmy standing up.

'Go on,' nodded Clarence.

'Could he do it with bitter and bottles of Guinness as well?'

'Do what, boy?' frowned Clarence Bristol.

'Turn water into bitter and bottles of Guinness, sir?'

'I er,' stuttered Clarence taken aback.

'Lot of boozers, weren't they, sir?' continued Jimmy.

'Sit down,' bawled Clarence angrily. 'You stupid brainless oaf,' he fumed as he closed his Bible with a flourish. 'Get out your arithmetic books,' he snapped as he put the Bible in his desk and then went to the blackboard.

The class then settled down to simple mathematical

problems under the glowering eyes of Clarence Bristol whose patience was again to be sorely tried before the finishing bell finally sounded.

After school a crowd of boys collected on the pavement outside the school gates. Among them were Johnny Crabb, Jimmy King, Terry and Peter Kelly, Georgie and Jackie Cloke, the Collins brothers and Johnny Vincent.

'Up ter no good mark my words,' said the caretaker with a sniff as he leaned on his broom watching them.

Clarence Bristol, who was standing next to him nodded. 'You may have a point Mr Turner,' he conceded. 'No doubt I will be informed in due course,' he said in a superior manner and then turned and walked back into school. The caretaker rolled his eyes and sniffed again. 'Pompous bleeder,' he muttered as he began to sweep the playground.

The Tennants lived in a terraced bay-windowed house in Watermill Street with virtually no front garden. The bay window was less than six feet from the three-foot high garden wall which was now minus its wrought iron railings, these having been taken for the war effort a year previously.

Albert Tennant was the second engineer on a large cargo vessel and he had brought home the pineapple, oranges and bananas on his last leave. Now they stood proudly adorning the bay window in a bright yellow dish placed in the centre of a Victorian mahogany stand that filled the small bay window. The pineapple stood up, flanked by the oranges and bananas like some coat of arms for all to see. It gave Doris Tennant some satisfaction when she heard the children out on the pavement as she was sure that it was the only pineapple in Hythe and being the owner of it filled her with some importance.

The children would have seen her if she had gone into the front room as she had taken down her lace curtains in order to give anyone passing by an unobstructed view of her fruit, so she went into the hall and stood near the front door in order to hear the comments of the children, and she did not have long to wait.

'It's a queer lookin' bleedin' thing aint it?' observed Johnny Crabb, as he sat on her wall.

'Aye,' agreed Georgie Cloke. 'Can yer eat it?'

'Corse yer can,' said Johnny, 'my mum says yer can.'

'Still think it looks like a shrunken 'ead,' said Terry Kelly, who was now sitting on the wall next to Johnny.

'Yer right,' nodded Johnny in agreement.

'Maybe it's old Ma Tennant's?' he said reflectively.

'Could be old Ma Tennant's, maybe old Tennant's dun 'er in,' said Terry Kelly with a grin.

'My mum said her old man only went ter sea ter get away from 'er nagging.'

In the hall Doris Tennant's face went red as she cocked her ear to the door in order to hear more clearly, breathing deeply as she did so.

'I took my great Aunt Alice a cup of tea yesterday morning,' said Jimmy King, 'er 'ead looked like that as she sat up in bed.'

'Not surprised,' remarked Johnny, peering at the fruit, 'she's an ugly old cow anyway.'

'My big sister looks like that when she goes ter bed,' said Georgie Cloke with a grin.

'She's bloody 'orrible too,' retorted Johnny.

'Hey Johnny,' said Billy Collins, 'd'yer think she'll give us a bit if we ask?'

'Might,' replied Johnny hopefully as he jumped off the wall. He bounded to the neat front door in the centre of which was a highly polished door knocker.

It was unfortunate for Doris Tennant that her ear was almost on the other side of the large door knocker. Johnny Crabb gave the knocker a resounding thump and it could be heard all down the street; to Doris Tennant, whose eardrum was inches from it the noise was akin to a bomb exploding. Her dentures seemed to rattle and when it occurred again she almost staggered away from the door. At last she regained her composure, then the knocker landed again as she turned the lock and opened the door.

'Are you trying to knock my door down?' she demanded angrily of a grinning Johnny Crabb.

'Thought you couldn't 'ear, going deaf like,' he began.

'What do you want?' she asked hostilely.

'Can we 'ave a bit of your pineapple?' asked Johnny.

'No, you cannot,' she glared as she slammed the front door in his face.

Undeterred, Johnny Crabb pushed open the letter box and shouted into it.

'Bleeding show off, yer mean ole cow.'

'Well!' exploded Doris Tennant, her face now bright red with anger. Before she could open the door again the door knocker landed with a force that rattled the windows. When she opened the door at last she could hear the sound of running feet and by the time she had reached the pavement Johnny Crabb and company were halfway down the street. Doris was about to shout after them but she saw a grinning neighbour on the other side of the street who had obviously enjoyed the whole episode.

Breathing deeply and muttering under her breath she went back into her house. Within an hour the lace curtains were back at the bay window and the pineapple no longer on view.

5

Though Johnny Crabb was always in trouble at school and in endless scrapes out of it, at home there was no better boy. Good with his younger sisters he was always helping his mother who supplemented the meagre family allowances of a private soldier with two cleaning jobs.

In the morning she would be up early to clean the nearby baker's shop and in the evening the offices of a small brewery situated near the centre of the town.

Johnny had a firewood round, and he would spend hours chopping up wood in their yard and his sisters would bundle it together and tie it with string.

He was always on the scrounge for wood and would ask all the grocers in the town each week if they had any empty butter boxes. Half the money he made he gave to his mother who was very glad of it, and he always gave his sisters money each week for helping him.

From the profits of his firewood round one week Johnny bought himself a fishing float. It was an imposing float: a bulbous cork painted red and green with a quill painted red and white going right through it. The top had a spot of luminous paint which made it distinguishable in the dark.

'It's a smasher,' said Johnny as he took it out of a brown paper bag and held it up.

'Cor, look at that,' said Jimmy as Johnny handed it to him.

'Don't drop it, Kingy,' said Johnny anxiously.

'Nar, ain't it smashing,' said Jimmy again.

'You'll need a brick ter make it cock,' said Terry Kelly, a trace of envy in his voice.

'Got a box of weights,' said Johnny triumphantly. He shook the tin of lead weights he had been carrying. 'Come on, let's go down ter the canal and try it.'

'Alright,' agreed Jimmy.

'Got to be 'ome by six,' said Terry.

'Plenty of time,' said Johnny, picking up his bamboo cane.

The Crabbs lived in a little stone cottage near the lifeboat station and to get to the canal they had to pass the lifeboat station and the assortment of boats on the shingle near it. Two elderly fishermen were repairing their nets and they looked up as the boys approached them.

'Hallo, Mr Darkie,' said Johnny.

'Hallo Johnny, going fishing?' replied the fisherman.

'Yeh, wanna see my new float?' said Johnny who pulled the brown paper bag containing the float from his pocket and proudly presented it.

'My, that's a bonny float,' said George Dark with a grin.

'Catch a shark with that,' chuckled the second fisherman.

'There aint none in the canal,' sniffed Terry Kelly.

'Yer never know what comes in when those sluices are open at Seabrook. I've seen a skate in the canal before now,' said George Dark sagely nodding his head.

'Mr Darkie, you ain't seen my dad's ship 'ave yer?' said Jimmy.

The old coastguard-cum-fisherman blinked his eyes as he spoke. 'Er, no son I haven't.' The disappointment on the boy's face touched the old man. 'Look Jimmy, if I see it going by I'll come straight to your Aunt's pub and tell you, how's that?' he smiled.

'Cor, thanks Mr Darkie,' beamed Jimmy.

'Come on Kingy,' yelled a now distant Johnny Crabb.

'Bye, Mr Darkie,' said Jimmy as he ran off.

George Dark looked at his companion and shrugged. 'What can you say to these kids,' he mumbled.

His companion nodded. 'Three right tearaways there keep old Bristol on his toes I'll be bound.'

'That's a fact,' agreed George Dark as he expertly finished a hole in his net.

At half past seven Jimmy and Terry left Johnny Crabb fishing near the Nelson bridge. There was a cool east wind and the fish had not been biting.

'I'm staying 'ere until it's dark. I wanna see my float in the dark,' said Johnny as Jimmy and Terry left him.

Jimmy came into the public bar by the side door. His great aunt's public house The North Star did not boast many regular customers and there were only three in the bar. At the little sink behind the bar his mother was washing some glasses. She looked up and gave him a hostile look.

'Where've you been?' she demanded.

'Down by the canal,' replied Jimmy.

'Mr Keeler has just been in, says some boys were in his garden, walking on his plants, and that you were one of them.'

'I ain't been in his garden,' protested Jimmy.

'He says you have and don't say ain't,' snapped his mother.

'I haven't,' said Jimmy.

'So there you are,' Great Aunt Alice, who was tall for a woman, loomed over him with her hair piled high on her head and long earrings swinging from the abnormally large lobes on her ears.

'And what have you to say for yourself?' boomed Aunt Alice.

'Nuffin,' replied Jimmy.

'Nothing, Mr Keeler's plants were trampled on by you and your friends and all you can say is nothing.'

'I ain't, er, I mean I haven't been in his garden,' replied Jimmy.

'One of our regular customers too my dear,' said Aunt Alice to his mother who was developing a nervous twitch in her neck. 'First customer every day always two pints of bitter sometimes three,' Aunt Alice droned on, giving Jimmy a glare from time to time.

'He has been to the police,' his mother's nervous twitch seemed to be getting worse, and suddenly her attention was on Jimmy. 'Get to bed you little beast,' she lashed out with her right hand catching Jimmy on the ear, the surprise of the blow almost knocked him over; instead he fell against some glasses.

'Watch what you are doing, boy,' boomed Aunt Alice.

His mother moved to strike him again, but Jimmy nimbly stepped out of her way and ran out of the bar and up the stairs to his bedroom.

He lay on his bed and thought about his father; if only he would come home, if only, if only. He got undressed and then got into bed, still thinking about his father's ship until he fell asleep.

The following morning after assembly Clarence Bristol called him out in front of the class. 'Mr Keeler of Stade Gardens has complained to the police and to the school that certain boys have done a lot of damage on his allotment and that you are one of them.'

'I wasn't, sir,' said Jimmy, shaking his head. At that moment Mr Alton entered the classroom.

'You were, King, don't tell lies,' snapped the headmaster. 'Mr Keeler saw you with his own eyes.'

'I wasn't, sir,' replied Jimmy.

'And who were the others, Crabb and Kelly?' persisted Mr Alton.

'No sir, none of us were,' protested Jimmy.

'May I borrow your cane Mr Bristol?'

'Certainly headmaster,' replied Clarence, almost bounding to his cupboard with eagerness.

'Hold out your hand, King,' said the headmaster, taking the proffered cane from Clarence Bristol.

'Right hand,' whack, whack, whack, the cane lashed his hand. 'Left hand,' again the cane came down remorselessly.

Jimmy's face was white but defiant and his eyes dry.

'Now go to your desk, King.' Mr Alton handed the cane back to Clarence Bristol and quickly left the classroom.

Johnny and Terry commiserated with him at playtime as he put his hands under the cold water tap.

'He laid 'em on,' said Johnny sympathetically.

'Yer and I weren't in old Keeler's garden or on his allotment,' sniffed Jimmy.

'We always get the blame,' said Terry disconsolately.

'Yeh, no matter wot 'appens,' agreed Johnny.

Jimmy had little to say for the rest of the day and his pals did not press him after what had happened, but a plan was forming in Jimmy's mind to get his own back on Mr Keeler.

His great aunt, in common with other licensees in the town had all her beer in barrels. There was no cellar in her pub and they were kept in the yard behind and put on the counter as required. Each small wooden barrel had a highly polished brass tap which was struck into the barrel under which was a container to catch the drips from the tap. There was a wooden bung in the top of the barrel to control the flow of beer and a neat cover was placed over the barrel. The containers when half full were emptied back into the barrel by means of a funnel and removing the bung in the top of the barrel.

Jimmy knew which barrel of bitter was in use and the fact that Mr Keeler was usually the first customer of the day. With this knowledge Jimmy decided to put something in the barrel and accordingly some days later when he had checked that the bitter barrel was almost empty he rose early and got a bottle from the garden shed.

He could hear his uncle and aunt snoring as he came back into the pub and creeping into the bar he climbed on a stool and removed the cover and the bung from the bitter barrel. He moved the barrel, there was not much in it. Carefully he emptied the bottle of thick brown liquid into the enamel funnel. The noise of it hitting the level of the bitter alarmed him and he stopped for a moment. There was silence. He then continued to pour until the thick brown liquid was almost gone. Quickly he replaced the bung and the cover then washed the funnel.

Having disposed of the bottle he crept back to bed, his heart thumping with excitement.

That morning before school he told Johnny Crabb what he had done.

'You won't tell anyone will yer, Crabbie?' said Jimmy anxiously.

'Nar, God's honour,' replied Johnny.

Jimmy told him what he had done and Johnny started to laugh. 'You put liquid 'orse shit in it?' said Johnny.

'Yeah, I mixed it up and strained it through my aunt's silver tea strainer ter get rid of the bits.'

'Ha ha ha,' chortled Johnny, 'that'll shake him,' he gurgled.

Before school that morning Mr Alton had a visitor. It was Mr Keeler of Stade Gardens

'I caught some boys yesterday evening on my allotment; three to be exact: a Peter Ball, James White and Edward Wood.'

'Indeed? And was James King among them?' asked Mr Alton.

'Ah yes, I made a mistake there, these boys admitted it was them the last time,' said Mr Keeler.

'I see,' said Mr Alton. 'I am grateful to you for telling me.'

'I've told Mr Bristol of my mistake and he said it's swings and roundabouts with boys,' smiled Mr Keeler.

'Er, yes,' replied the headmaster, inwardly annoyed at the cavalier attitude of his most senior member of staff.

'Thank you again for telling me,' said Mr Alton as he escorted Mr Keeler from his office.

He returned to his office and sat down heavily. He had caned a boy unjustly but how could he apologise to a boy of his age? 'Swings and roundabouts,' he muttered as he thought of Clarence Bristol's cynical remark and shook his head.

The school bell rang and another day had begun for him.

Promptly on opening time Cuthbert Keeler entered the public bar of The North Star Inn.

'Good morning Mr Keeler, pint of bitter?' asked Mrs King brightly.

'Yes, thank you Ruby.'

Ruby King turned on the tap of the bitter barrel and the amber liquid flowed into a pint tankard, whilst Cuthbert Keeler, puffing at a new briar, watched appreciatively.

'There we are,' said Ruby King as she placed the tankard on the counter in front of him.

'Thank you, my dear,' he said, handing her a half a crown. He lifted the tankard and drank deeply, a frown appeared on his face as he lowered the tankard.

'Anything wrong Cuthbert?' enquired Ruby anxiously as she gave him his change.

He smacked his lips, 'I think its this new briar pipe leaving a funny taste in my mouth, always do you know, a new pipe.'

'Oh I see,' smiled Ruby.

He finished his pint and ordered another. Having had three pints he left the pub and commenced to do his shopping.

By four he had stomach ache, and for the next twenty four hours was rarely out of the toilet. The doctor, when consulted, diagnosed a gastric disorder.

When Mr Keeler's indisposition was mentioned at the meal table some days later Jimmy smiled but said nothing.

6

Jimmy knew that his father was out in the Far East, and that his ship, a cruiser, had been there for over a year now. He was beginning to forget what he looked like.

Two weeks after the incident with Mr Keeler his mother received a telegram from the Admiralty in London. Her husband's ship had been sunk and there had been only a handful of survivors. Petty Officer Jack King they regretted to inform her had not been one of them. Ruby King took the news well, not the least because she was being comforted by a sergeant from nearby Shorncliffe army camp.

The morning of the day that the news arrived Johnny Crabb had called for Jimmy on his way to school. He came through the back yard and knocked on the kitchen door. Jimmy opened the door and frowned at him.

'You're early?' he said curiously.

'Yeah,' agreed Johnny.

From past experience Jimmy knew that when Johnny Crabb arrived early for school he was in some kind of scrape. They went out into the yard and Jimmy closed the kitchen door.

'I'm goin',' called Jimmy but there was no reply.

'I've made a football out of rags,' said Jimmy. He pointed to a bundle of rags tied up with white string that lay near two empty beer barrels which had been placed against the kitchen wall.

'That's my goal,' said Jimmy, pointing to the two empty beer barrels as Johnny Crabb pounced on the makeshift football.

'You get in goal,' said Johnny as he took a kick at the bundle.

'Alright,' agreed Jimmy, and he stood between the barrels.

Above the barrels was the kitchen window, the top casement being open six inches to allow the cat to get in and out.

'I'm Tommy Lawton,' said Johnny, taking a run at the rag football. It flew from his boot and went over Jimmy's head to land with a thud against the top casement window. Jimmy turned and looked up at the window as the makeshift football fell at his feet. Two large cracks had appeared in the window and a large dirty mark had been left by the football.

'Cor bli,' gasped Jimmy in alarm.

'Aw shit,' said Johnny. 'Still, it ain't busted it proper,' he said philosophically.

'My aunt'll play up when she sees it,' said Jimmy miserably.

'Can't yer say the cat did it?' suggested Johnny helpfully.

'The cat?' said Jimmy, frowning.

'Yer, the cat could 'ave drunk some of this beer that's been spilled from these barrels.'

'Nar,' sniffed Jimmy, 'my aunt'll never believe the cat did it when it came 'ome pissed.'

They could suddenly hear a noise in the kitchen.

'It's my Uncle Frank,' hissed Jimmy as he picked up the rag football and hid it under some beer crates.

They slipped stealthily out of the yard and quietly closed the gate. After a few paces they broke into a run, not stopping until they came in sight of the school gates.

'I've an idea,' puffed Johnny as they relaxed into a walk.' They crossed the road and Terry Kelly raced towards them.

'I've got 'em,' he announced excitedly.

'What?' queried Johnny.

'My mum's silk bloomers, that's what,' replied Terry breathlessly.

"Ave yer?' grinned Johnny as they entered the school playground. 'We can make a parachute then,' he said happily.

The school bell rang and they lined up in their respective classes on a coloured line, each class having its own colour. Clarence Bristol walked up and down the lines and then to the gate to spot any latecomers.

'No talking in the lines,' he rapped. 'Miss Darrowfield's class lead on then Mrs Woolett's.' The children then filed into school for prayers and assembly. Afterwards they dispersed to their respective classrooms where Clarence Bristol was later engaged in trying to impart his wisdom to his class.

'Now who can tell me what our town is called?' he said, standing in front of the class and still wearing his bicycle clips.

'Hythe, sir,' shouted Johnny Crabb, his arm in the air.

'We know that, you brainless boy, what else? A special name, come on, tell me,' snapped Clarence impatiently.

'A stink port sir,' said Jimmy King putting up his hand.

'Yees,' said Mr Bristol uncertainly. 'A cinq port you mean, pronounced sank not stink, King,' he continued benignly. 'The French word *cinq* meaning five, the five ports.'

'My mum says it stinks sir,' retorted Jimmy quickly.

Before Clarence Bristol could reply there was a knock on the classroom door and a small girl entered.

'Please sir, Mr Alton wants to see King sir.'

Clarence nodded. 'King to the headmaster, hurry,' he snapped looking hard at Jimmy.

Jimmy left his desk his heart thumping. 'Now what?' he thought. That bitter barrel had been emptied over three weeks ago, so it could not be that. Was it the window?

The headmaster smiled as he entered his office, 'Ah er King, come in,' he paused and looked at the school register tracing the names with his forefinger. 'It's James isn't it,' he said quietly.

Jimmy nodded. He seemed to have lost his voice, such treatment seemed so out of place at school.

'Er, I have something your mother has asked me to tell you my boy,' the headmaster, a kindly man at heart, felt distinctly uncomfortable. Just three weeks ago he had caned the boy for something he had not done, now it fell to him to have to break the news to him of his father's death.

He licked his thin lips, uncertain how to begin. Jimmy stood with his hands behind his back, his heart still thumping.

'James I'm sorry to have to tell you that your mother has just been informed that your father has been killed in action.'

'Sir,' muttered Jimmy.

'I'm very sorry my boy, your father died at sea fighting for his king and country.'

As the words sank in Jimmy's face began to screw up. He clenched his fists as tears began to run down his face. The headmaster averted his eyes.

'He ain't sir, he's comin 'ome, he promised me,' sobbed Jimmy. 'It's 'cos of the kitchen winder, thats what it is.'

The headmaster stood up, uncertain what to do. He put his hand into his pocket and took out a penny.

'Here James, go and get yourself a cake and go fishing, I'm always seeing you fishing by the Nelson bridge.'

'Don't want a cake I want my dad,' sobbed Jimmy, ignoring the headmaster's outstretched hand. He turned and ran out of the office down the corridor and out through the school playground. He squeezed through the railings as the caretaker had locked the gate and hared off down the road. The headmaster looked out of his office window and watched him go, making no attempt to follow. He took out his handkerchief and blew his nose, then walked out of his office and down the corridor to Mr Bristol's class.

Clarence Bristol was endeavouring with little success to explain to Johnny Crabb where rain came from when Mr Alton entered the classroom. Quickly he explained to Clarence what had happened.

'If he does not return within the hour send Crabb to look for him. I think it best he went fishing, he's always at it, let Crabb go with him. They are invariably together.'

'Yes, headmaster,' replied Clarence Bristol.

Jimmy was sitting on the parapet of the Red Lion square bridge when Johnny Crabb eventually found him some two hours later. He was not fishing but looking aimlessly in the water.

Johnny had two bamboo canes in one hand and a brown paper bag in the other.

'Hi Kingy, I brought yer rod,' said Johnny as he sat down on the parapet next to him. 'And yer aunt sent this, it's a sandwich and an apple,' said Johnny, giving him the paper bag.

Jimmy brushed the palm of his hand over his tear-stained face and nodded. Bad news or not he felt hungry. He took the paper bag and opened it. The sandwich tasted good. He stared at the water as he ate, not wishing his friend to see his tear-stained face.

''Ere, I've something for yer,' said Johnny holding out his hand.

Jimmy half turned his head. In Johnny's grubby hand was his prized float.

''Ere, you 'ave it,' said Johnny.

'Nar, I can't take that,' replied Jimmy knowing how hard Johnny had saved for it.

'Yeah, take it, I'm gettin' another.' Johnny pushed the float into Jimmy's hand. 'Come on let's do some fishin', you gotta catch some fish fer Charlie the drayman's cat haven't yer?'

Jimmy nodded. Charlie was one of his regular customers and always gave him a sixpence. Soon they were fishing.

Johnny eyed him from time to time but did not speak until Jimmy unexpectedly confided, 'He's comin' home Crabby, he is 'e promised.'

Johnny nodded understandingly. 'If 'e promised 'e will. My dad's goin ter build me a boat when 'e gets 'ome, 'e promised too so we could all go fishin' in it, you, me, your dad and my dad,' enthused Johnny.

'Yeah, smashing,' replied Jimmy, his dirty tear-stained face now wreathed in smiles.

'Yeah, smashing,' he said again as he rubbed his knees together in excitement.

7

Making a miniature parachute was no easy matter as the boys soon found out. With Jimmy's mother's scissors and needle and cotton from one of Johnny's young sisters they sat in the shed behind the North Star Inn.

'Don't bloody cut, these scissors,' said Johnny disgustedly as he endeavoured to cut the gusset out of Mrs Kelly's silk underwear.

'Let me 'ave a go,' said Terry Kelly, grabbing at the white silk bloomers.

Meanwhile Mrs Kelly had now realised her loss.

'They were pegged securely to the line,' she muttered crossly to herself as she looked about her garden 'They couldn't have blown away, there's no wind, I'll bet it's that gypsy woman who called this morning.'

Convinced that was how her underwear had disappeared she reported the matter to the police. The station sergeant took the particulars without any comment or trace of a smile.

'There was no wind so they could not have blown away,' she said as the sergeant finished writing.

'We will look into the matter Mrs Kelly,' he said politely.

That evening when special constable Clarence Bristol reported for duty at the police station, the station sergeant raised the matter with him.

'A Mrs Kelly has had her underwear stolen constable.'

'Oh yes,' remarked Clarence cagily, aware that a regular constable was grinning at him.

'Aye, one of her boys is in your class I understand,'

said the sergeant, peering at him.

'Of that I am only too well aware,' said Clarence sourly.

'Look into the matter will you?' said the sergeant, putting on his helmet.

Clarence did not like the sergeant and neither lost the chance of baiting the other.

'Was she wearing them at the time sergeant?' asked Clarence, giving what passed in his case for a grin.

'Off her clothes line constable,' replied the sergeant sharply as he stooped to put on his bicycle clips, giving Clarence a glare as he did so.

With the help of Johnny's sister Jean they managed to make a parachute of sorts.

'It ain't sewn very well,' sniffed Terry as he pushed his fingers through one of the seams.

'She's only nine,' replied Johnny aggressively. 'If you'd cut it straight,' he said, holding up their effort which passed for a parachute.

'Clokey found another one last night,' said Jimmy morosely.

'Did 'e?' Johnny Crabb looked at Jimmy in disbelief.

'Yer, down by the scouts hut,' said Jimmy.

'I've seen it as well,' said Terry miserably.

'He won't swop it, I offered him my Mills bomb for it but he wouldn't,' he added.

'You've got a Mills bomb? Where is it?' demanded Johnny.

'Found it yesterday on the ranges,' said Terry. 'Couldn't take it 'ome with me, mum would have gone potty the mood she's in.'

'Where is it then?' asked Jimmy.

'Took it round ter my gran's. I've hidden it under her bed, she's got all sorts of boxes under it so she won't find it.'

'Ugh,' grunted Johnny as he held up the tattered object which was supposed to be a parachute.

'D'yer think it will work?' said Jimmy, looking at it doubtfully.

'Dunno,' replied Johnny as he tied a stone with a hole in it that he had found on the beach.

'Let's go and see,' said Johnny.

They left the shed and went out into the road. Johnny wrapped the parachute round the stone and ran down the road. Then he hurled it as far as he could up in the air. Unfortunately he erred in its direction and it came down in the garden of a detached house with a wall around it. As for opening like a parachute it went up like a stone and fell like one, and the sound of glass breaking gave the boys the first indication that it had landed.

'Aw shit, it didn't open,' grimaced Johnny.

'Sounds like it went through a bleeding greenhouse,' said Jimmy, starting to run.

Terry Kelly did not need any encouragement as he raced after Jimmy. Johnny Crabb however was not so lucky. The irate householder recognised him as he ran to catch up with his friends.

Later that day when Clarence reported to the police station the inspector called him into his office.

'We had a complaint today constable from a householder regarding damage to a conservatory window. An object was thrown through it. There it is.'

The inspector pointed at the erstwhile parachute and frowned. 'The owner of the property recognised one of the boys, a John Crabb, does the name ring a bell with you constable?'

'Ring a bell, inspector?' repeated Clarence grimacing. 'It gives me a positive headache.'

'Then I'll let you deal with the matter, it will save a lot of paperwork and I'm sure your methods are more effective than the courts,' smiled the Inspector, who appreciated what a boon Clarence was to them.

'Thank you sir, I will deal with it,' replied Clarence.

'Ah and you'll need this,' the inspector continued, holding up the parachute and stone.

As Clarence took it he said, 'And I'll see Mrs Kelly as well.'

'Mrs Kelly?' The inspector looked puzzled. 'Who—' he began.

'She had her underwear stolen, sir,' said the sergeant, who had just joined them.

'Oh!' murmured the inspector, frowning.

'Unless I miss my guess this was her underwear,' said Clarence, holding up the parachute.

The inspector started to chuckle and shook his head. 'Boys will be boys,' he murmured.

'They will indeed,' said Clarence, his eyes glinting.

The following morning Clarence and the headmaster discussed the matter before school commenced.

'I've seen Mrs Kelly headmaster and she confirms that the material is indeed from her, um, underwear.' Clarence had just informed Mr Alton of the sequence of events regarding the home-made parachute.

The headmaster breathed deeply and put the palms of his hands on his desk as he spoke. 'It's that boy Crabb, he's the ringleader.'

'Undoubtedly headmaster, though on this occasion Kelly was equally to blame. He did purloin the er, um…'

'Yes quite,' agreed Mr Alton.

'The point is the cane does not seem to deter Crabb.'

'I agree headmaster but what can we do?' said Clarence with a shrug.

'I know it's difficult. I'll think about it,' said the headmaster with a sigh.

The following morning Johnny Crabb and Terry Kelly were caned before the school after assembly. Clarence Bristol would have caned Jimmy too and he put it to Mr

Alton with some feeling. 'After all headmaster, he did aid and abet by letting them make the object at his home.'

Mr Alton agreed but bearing in mind past events and Mr Bristol's swings and roundabouts philosophy he forbade it and Jimmy was reprieved.

The incident made the boys more determined than ever to find a flare parachute. Every evening they would comb the night sky for signal flares but none seemed to fall in the area. Red and green flares could be seen at times out at sea, much to the boys disappointment.

Late one night, about eleven, Johnny Crabb woke up with a start. His little bedroom seemed to be bathed in a green light. 'A parachute flare,' he mumbled, instantly awake. He clambered out of bed and looked out of the window. Sure enough the flare was coming down close by, almost it seemed on the beach.

'Cor,' he muttered, pulling on his trousers. He watched to see where it had landed as he pulled on his socks.

'It's at the end of Stade Street,' he mumbled, grabbing his boots and jacket. Noiselessly he let himself out of the house and then put on his boots.

Soon he was on the seafront walking to the end of Stade Street. It was deserted and very dark. There was a quarter moon but the sky was full of cloud which obscured it from time to time. At the end of Stade Street he began his search but soon realised that without any light it was a hopeless task. He was about to return home when he spotted a bicycle outside a row of beach huts which were now no longer used. Stealthily he approached it. The door of the beach hut was partly open and he could hear voices coming from inside. He crept close. It sounded like a man and a woman.

'Hold still Mildred will you?' It was a man's voice and it was familiar.

'Ooh! Clarence,' said a female voice.

'That's 'im,' thought Johnny, 'it's Clarence Bristol with a woman and it's his bike.'

Johnny unscrewed the rear tyre cap and removed the valve. The air hissed out. Quickly he removed the valve rubber then replaced the valve and screwed on the cap. He had almost completed the operation on the front tyre when he heard Clarence say. 'I heard a noise outside.'

'Careful Clarence, you're standing on my knickers,' said the female voice.

'Someone's interfering with my bike,' exclaimed Clarence.

'Perhaps it's a German paratrooper,' came the woman's sarcastic comment.

Johnny did not wait any longer, He ran off into the darkness as fast as his legs could carry him.

Clarence came out of the hut followed by Mildred Pullen.

'There's your bike, still there,' said Mildred, peering into the gloom.

'Aye but who was that running off, that's what I'd like to know?' said Clarence, who as yet had not noticed that his tyres were flat.

He eventually arrived back at the station over a half an hour late, having spent some time trying to pump up his tyres and only giving up when the pump became too hot to hold. He pushed his bicycle back to the police station and it did not help his temper when the sergeant asked him if he had got lost.

'About to send out a search party, constable,' he said jovially. Clarence ignored him and signed out. He would find the culprit if it was the last thing he ever did.

The following morning he gave his class an even closer scrutiny. His prime suspect was Crabb, but he was working industriously for a change.

Clarence peered at the class. Was anyone yawning, that was what he was looking for, anyone who persistently yawned. None of the boy's were, only Mavis Pullen had yawned.

He looked at her carefully. It could not have been Mavis, he decided. Whoever ran away could run fast and Mavis was far too fat to do that.

He dismissed her from his mind. It could be one of his police colleagues but it was highly unlikely, though he would not have put it past one or two of them.

It puzzled and worried him a little that someone knew his little secret, so careful had they been, even Mildred's daughter Mavis knew nothing, or did she?

The day ended with Clarence no nearer catching the culprit, and with these thoughts in his mind he made his way home.

8

One afternoon when Jimmy arrived home from school he was surprised to find his Great Aunt Alice looking around the yard with a frown on her face. It seemed she was searching for something. When she spotted Jimmy coming in through the gate she ceased her search and beckoned to him.

'Yes, Aunt Alice,' said Jimmy anxiously.

Aunt Alice looked down at him. She was tall for a woman and her grey hair which was piled up on her head in a style that was popular forty years previously seemed to add to her height.

'I have been looking for my empty crates,' she said, looking at him severely. 'The brewers were here this morning and there should have been at least ten to go back and we could only find one. What do you know about it?' She stood there with her hands on her hips and Jimmy could see that she was annoyed. 'I have better things to do than look for my beer crates.'

As Jimmy was well aware she always had a lie down every afternoon and the loss of her nap had not improved her temper.

'I don't know, Aunt Alice,' said Jimmy with a shrug. 'I 'aven't seen 'em,' he replied truthfully.

'Earlier this week they were piled up against the wall over there,' Aunt Alice pointed to the yard wall. A sudden unpleasant thought occurred to Jimmy. It dawned on him where they could have gone; Johnny Crabb had come into the yard some days previously and had looked at the crates but said nothing. In his unceasing search for wood he must have come back and taken them to chop up for firewood.

'There was a deposit of five shillings on all those crates,' snapped Aunt Alice, 'and I want them returned as soon as possible. I've no doubt that it is one of your friends who has taken them, and if they are not returned there will be trouble.' She turned and walked back into the kitchen, leaving Jimmy standing there with his mouth slightly open.

He hurried into the kitchen after her. 'I ain't 'ad them, honest Aunt Alice I ain't touched them,' he began.

She heaved a sigh as she looked at him, slowly shaking her head.

'Perhaps you have not, and do stop saying ain't, it irritates me. I am sure you can find out who has had them, so you can go now and look for them and there is no tea until you find and return them, do you understand?'

Jimmy shrugged his shoulders and left the kitchen. He knew that if Johnny Crabb had taken them they would now be in pieces, if not already burnt by one of his firewood customers. Still hoping that he might retrieve some of them he hurried out of the yard and made his way towards the Crabbs' cottage. Jimmy could hear wood being chopped as he went round the back of the cottage and sure enough Johnny was sitting on a large stone chopping up some crates.

'Eh,' said Jimmy pointing at the crates that were stacked behind Johnny, 'they're my aunt's crates and I want 'em back,' he said in a loud voice.

Johnny stopped chopping and looked up at him. 'They bloody ain't your aunt's crates, these are from the Risin' Sun,' replied Johnny aggressively.

'Well what 'ave yer done wiv 'er crates?'

'I ain't 'ad 'er bloody crates,' snapped Johnny.

'Oh yes you 'ave. I know you and I want 'em back, anyway they look like 'er crates over there,' said Jimmy, pointing at the crates stacked behind Johnny. 'They've got Whitbread on 'em.'

'I told yer they're from the bloody Risin' Sun,' said Johnny, his face going red with anger.

At that moment the back door opened and a harassed Mrs Crabb appeared.

'Whats all this noise for?' she said quickly.

'It's my aunt, Mrs Crabb,' said Jimmy quickly. He knew with Johnny you had to get in first.

'She's been playing up over 'er beer crates, he's 'ad 'em and there's a deposit of five shillings on 'em and she wants 'em back, and she said I don't get any tea til I get 'em.'

'You'd better give them back Johnny if you had them, we don't want any trouble, what about those over there?' Mrs Crabb pointed at some crates in the far corner of the shingled garden.

'They ain't from his aunt's pub,' said Johnny, 'they're from the Rifleman's Arms.'

'I don't care where they came from,' said Mrs Crabb with an air of resignation, 'give them back to Jimmy.'

'Alright,' muttered Johnny, 'you can 'ave them over there,' he nodded at the crates belonging to the licensee of the Rifleman's Arms.

'Are yer goin ter 'elp me carry 'em?' said Jimmy.

'No I bloody ain't,' retorted Johnny as he began to chop up a crate.

'Go and help him Johnny,' said Mrs Crabb as she turned and went back into the cottage.

Johnny put down his axe and reluctantly got to his feet.

'My mum will be on ter me over this,' growled Johnny as he glared at Jimmy.

'It ain't my bloody fault, I've 'ad my aunt on ter me and I know nuffing about it,' replied Jimmy abruptly.

'Um,' Johnny grunted, 'come on.' He picked up four crates and Jimmy picked up a further four and followed Johnny out of the Crabbs' windswept garden.

Later when they sat down for their evening meal Jimmy mentioned the beer crates to his Aunt Alice.

'I've got your beer crates Aunt Alice, they are stacked out in the yard again.'

She looked at him over the top of her glasses as she replied. 'I am very pleased to hear it young man,' she said quietly. 'I need hardly ask where they came from or who had them,' she added pointedly.

'Well they're back now, I didn't know he took 'em,' shrugged Jimmy.

'He's not good company for you,' said his mother, her nervous twitch suddenly becoming pronounced. 'I've told you before that boy is always in trouble.'

Jimmy said nothing as he ate his tea and looked at his aunt.

'We'll say no more about the matter,' said Aunt Alice firmly. 'They have been returned and I am satisfied.'

Jimmy was about to say that they had come from the Rifleman's Arms but checked himself in time, deeming it wiser to say nothing about the matter.

His mother and Aunt Alice began talking about a film that was to be shown the following week at the Ritz cinema. Jimmy had seen the trailer and had not been impressed The film was about the birth of a baby. It was an adult only film and even if he wished it he wouldn't have been allowed into the cinema.

'I think I'll go and see it, Ruby,' said Aunt Alice, who rarely went to the cinema. 'What about you?'

'Yes I'd like to see it too,' replied Ruby King.

'He cannot see it,' said Aunt Alice looking at Jimmy.

'No of course not auntie,' replied Ruby.

'Don't want ter see it,' said Jimmy quickly. 'Saw some

of it on the trailer, rotten film,' he sniffed. 'About some old woman with 'er legs up in the air.'

'Good heavens, Ruby,' gasped Aunt Alice, a horrified look on her face. 'He's seen some already.'

Uncle Frank had burst out laughing, impervious to a stern look from Aunt Alice.

'There's a cowboy film on with it Aunt Alice,' said Jimmy helpfully.

'I am not interested in cowboy films,' said Aunt Alice severely. 'I shall leave before it begins.'

'Oh!' murmured Jimmy.

What a waste he thought, what a rotten waste.

Accompanied by Johnny Crabb and Terry Kelly, Jimmy sat on the canal bank by the Nelson bridge. They watched their floats in silence until at last Johnny spoke.

'Fink I've gotta bite.'

'Yeah looks like it,' agreed Jimmy as he raised his bamboo cane in an effort to bring his own float out of some weed.

'Bloody sweet ration goin' down again,' sniffed Terry miserably. 'From next week.'

'Is it?' Johnny Crabb's head turned sharply, his interest in his float now completely gone.

'Who said so?' he demanded aggressively.

''Eard it on the news at dinner time,' replied Terry miserably.

'It's only three ounces now,' said Jimmy with a frown. 'What's it goin' down to?'

'Two ounces,' replied Terry glumly.

'Bloody 'ell,' sniffed Johnny, a look of concern on his freckled face.

''Ow we supposed ter manage on that?' he demanded.

Jimmy shrugged his shoulders and shook his head. 'Dunno,' he said dolefully.

The news was regarded by the boys as nothing short of a calamity, battles that were taking place in Russia and North Africa were of little interest or concern to them, air raids were no more than a nuisance but the cutting of the sweet ration was a major disaster.

'I've 'ad me week's ration already and it's only bloody Tuesday,' said Johnny as he raised his bamboo and lifted his float out of the water. 'It's 'ad me bait,' he snapped as he grabbed at his hook. ''Ave you got any coupons Kingy?'

Jimmy shook his head. 'Nope,' he sniffed.

'Used mine on Sunday,' he replied.

'Thought you would 'ave 'ad plenty,' said Johnny with a note of accusation in his voice. 'With three grown-ups in your house.'

'Don't give me their sweet coupons do they?' replied Jimmy, his voice rising. 'Waste them on chocolate creams don't they?'

'Chocolate creams?' repeated Johnny, a frown on his face.

'Yeah my aunt likes chocolate peppermint creams. Bloody waste of coupons if yer ask me,' he said despondently.

Terry Kelly nodded his head in agreement.

'Thought she liked whisky?' remarked Johnny as he squeezed a piece of dough onto his hook.

'She does,' agreed Jimmy 'but she likes chocolate peppermint creams as well, so does my mum, a small box is three week's ration.' His voice rose as he thought of the waste.

'Yer could get at least twelve gobstoppers and four ounces of lemonade powder for that,' observed Johnny Crabb despondently.

'And two ounces of 'undreds and thousands,' added Jimmy.

They continued fishing in silence, eyes glued to their floats. At last Terry broke the silence.

'Clokey's making some,' he announced.

There was no reaction for a moment to his words.

''E's what?' Johnny Crabb's head jerked sideways to face Terry. 'Makin' some,' repeated Terry Kelly coolly.

'Makin' what?' demanded Johnny.

'Sweet coupons, that's what,' said Terry patiently.

''Ows he doin' that?' asked Jimmy, as his head also turned to face Terry Kelly.

'He's got a John Bull printing outfit that's what,' replied Terry.

'So's Kingy but he ain't made any sweet coupons,' sniffed Johnny.

'Didn't know yer could make sweet coupons with it,' said Jimmy, a frown on his face.

'Well yer know now,' retorted Johnny.

'Anyway I ain't got it,' sniffed Jimmy.

'Where is it then?' demanded Johnny

'You should know,' replied Jimmy aggressively. 'It's your fault I ain't got it.'

'My fault!' protested Johnny.

'Yes you,' snapped Jimmy. 'Before Christmas after we went carol singing and shared out the money in the private bar and you got hold of my John Bull printing outfit.'

'Oh that,' said Johnny in an offhand manner.

'What 'appened?' asked Terry curiously.

'He stamped words on the wall of the bar and they wouldn't come off,' jerking a thumb at Johnny.

'What words?' said Terry as Johnny started to laugh.

'Horse shit,' replied Jimmy. 'And it ain't bloody funny.'

'Horse shit,' laughed Terry, 'is that all?'

'Ain't it bleedin' enough,' Jimmy's voice was rising in anger. 'All over the wall! My aunt went potty when she saw it.'

'She's potty anyway,' sniffed Johnny, 'the ugly old cow.'

'She won't 'ave him in the place any more,' continued

Jimmy with feeling. 'Says you're not to darken her door again.'

'I ain't touched her doors the lying ole cow,' said Johnny angrily.

'That's wot she said,' said Jimmy emphatically.

'A bleeding liberty I call it. I get blamed fer everything.' Johnny's face went red as he spoke.

The boys relapsed into silence with thoughts on Georgie Cloke and his sweet coupon manufacturing operation.

Jimmy caught a small roach which he methodically took from his hook and put into his fishing bag. He re-baited his hook and cast out his line.

'The paper in ration books is different,' said Jimmy suddenly.

'What?' said Johnny.

'The paper sweet coupons are made of, I ain't seen any like it.' Johnny looked at Jimmy then at Terry Kelly.

'He's right, I ain't seen any either,' said Johnny with a frown.

'Where does Clokey get it from then?'

'He's being confirmed ain't he,' said Terry with a shrug.

'Wot are you bleedin' on about?' Johnny's answer was now aggressive, he was beginning to think Terry was taking the rise out of him. 'Wot's Clokey bein' confirmed got ter do wiv it eh?'

'He's got the paper from church,' explained Terry.

'From church,' repeated Jimmy.

'Yer, from those new missionary books they 'ave there, he nicks some of the pages out of them, the paper's the same,' explained Terry.

'The crafty bleeder,' gasped Johnny with ill concealed admiration in his voice.

''Ave you seen these missionary books?' asked Johnny as he knew that Terry was taken to church each week by his mother.

'Nar, our church doesn't 'ave them I've looked,' replied Terry.

'Only C of E I think, we're Catholics, you're C of E aren't yer Crabbie?'

'Yer, but we never go ter church,' replied Johnny.

'What about you Kingy?' said Johnny, turning to Jimmy.

' I dunno,' said Jimmy, 'I've never known my mum or aunt go ter church.'

'Yer must be C of E then,' said Johnny, 'like me.'

'Can't you two go to confirmation classes like Clokey?' suggested Terry.

Both Johnny and Jimmy looked at Terry in amazement.

'Me?' gasped Johnny, 'not bloody likely.'

'Or me,' said Jimmy in tones of horror.

'Anyway who would take Clokey's coupons, most shops won't accept loose coupons, only two sweet shops I know of will. The one next to the Ritz and old Ma Howden's. My mum won't even let me touch the ration books.'

'Nor mine,' agreed Jimmy.

'Old Ma Howden will take 'em, and she's busted 'er glasses, can't see proper, that's why she took Clokey's coupons,' explained Terry. Johnny and Jimmy were for once lost for words; the sheer brilliance of Georgie Cloke's plan had taken their breath away. Johnny slowly shook his head in wonderment as he murmured, 'And I thought Clokey was as thick as pig shit, it's bloody choice ter know.'

'If yer goin' ter do anything it'll 'ave ter be before old Ma Howden gets her glasses mended.'

'Aye,' Johnny agreed, nodding his head slowly.

'You'll 'ave ter go to confirmation classes, its the only way to get 'old of those missionary books, they are kept in the same room the vicar has the classes,' said Terry.

'Bloody 'ell fire,' moaned Johnny, 'I suppose we'll 'ave ter too won't we Kingy?' Johnny looked sidelong.

'I dunno,' said Jimmy as he moved his float away from some weed.

'Whadyer mean yer dunno?' demanded Johnny. 'If I go you go, that's only fair ain't it?'

'It's my John Bull printing outfit,' began Jimmy.

'Yer but,' Johnny paused, 'it's no bleeding good without the paper is it?'

'No but you need my printing outfit,' agreed Jimmy.

'Yer, but I'm not goin on me own,' said Johnny as he hunched his shoulders.

Terry and Jimmy exchanged glances, they knew their pal, he would not budge.

'Why don't you go, Kingy?' suggested Terry. 'Once yer 'ave the paper no need ter go again.'

'Yer, once we 'ave the paper sod it,' said Johnny, his face brightening.

'Alright then,' said Jimmy grudgingly, 'if it's only fer once.'

'You'd better get on to it straight away,' said Terry as he pulled his line out of the water.

'Why?' Johnny glared at him.

'Cos I told yer old Ma Howden's glasses fer one thing, and they only 'ave so many at confirmation classes, yer could be sent down ter the church hall and there ain't none there, Johnny Vincent found that out.'

'Cor bli,' began Johnny as his brow furrowed. 'Ow many are on ter this?'

'Dunno,' replied Terry.

'There's Jimmy Pierce, Charlie Reeves, Micky Mason even old Luggell Pump is goin.'

'Luggell Pump,' glared Johnny 'that bloody fool, anyway he's left school.'

They were referring to a youth named Timothy Keen who had a facial deformity that caused him to talk out of the corner of his mouth, added to which he had a stutter. All the boys called him Luggel Pump, those that would face him in a fight, such as Johnny, Jimmy and Terry who would often take on lads much older than themselves and win.

'Aye but he can still go ter confirmation classes,' said Terry.

'Have they got a John Bull printing outfit?' asked Jimmy.

'Nar, Clokey's been hiring his out and chargin' sixpence a day.'

'Bloody 'ell!' gasped Jimmy.

'You'd better get yours back, mate,' said Johnny as he pulled in his line.

'Has anyone besides Clokey taken coupons ter old Ma Howden?'

'His brothers 'ave and the two Collins, they live next door ter the Clokes,' replied Terry.

'We know that,' said Johnny impatiently. 'Who else?'

'Micky and Johnny Mason, Smelly Potter, Fatty Baker and there's...'

Johnny stopped him in full flow. 'Yer mean 'alf Hythe are on to it, by the time we get our coupons printed she'll 'ave no bleeding sweets left.'

'Or got her glasses mended, that's why I said yer got ter get a move on,' replied Terry.

Johnny stood up, grabbed his line and pushed the hook into the end of his bamboo cane.

'I'm goin 'ome now ter see me mum. I'll 'ave ter get a note from 'er, so will you Kingy.'

Jimmy stood up and pulled in his float and turned to Johnny.

'Yer,' he nodded, 'it's tea-time now. I'll ask me mum.'

'See yer up on the seafront later,' said Johnny as they made their way up the canal bank to Stade Street.

Aunt Alice and Uncle Frank were for once in a good mood when he arrived home for tea. They had been to the point to point races at Aldington and had a successful day. Uncle Frank had a small wholesale vegetable business and knew many of the farmers in the area, some of whom owned point to point horses. This gave him access to reliable information about the horses, and their capabilities, and since there were never more than five in a race the favourite invariably won. In one case that day however it had not and Uncle Frank and Aunt Alice had backed the outsider at four to one and it had won.

'Knew the favourite would lose. Old Bill Saunders told me he was saving it for Wye races to get a better price. Four winners eh! Not bad,' he chuckled.

Uncle Frank was looking bleary eyed already and it was barely five. He took a gulp of his whisky, put the glass down on the dining table with a thud and then belched, 'Manners'.

Aunt Alice ignored him as she put a plate of bread and butter on the table. 'Have you washed your hands young man?' she said, peering at Jimmy who sat in silence at the other end of the table.

'Yes, Aunt Alice,' he replied.

Aunt Alice nodded, her long earrings swaying as she did so. Jimmy watched them, fascinated.

The meal commenced and Jimmy, biding his time, decided to wait a short while before making his requests.

Other than their good fortune at the races the subject of conversation was the Licensed Victuallers annual ball.

'You'll need a new dress Ruby,' said Aunt Alice, looking at her niece over the top of her glasses.

Jimmy looked at his mother as he ate his bread, thinly spread with butter and jam.

'Yes I've put on a little weight just lately,' replied Ruby King as she helped herself to more potatoes.

His mother and aunt had their main meal in the evening before the pub opened and as Jimmy at the present time had a school dinner all he was given was bread and jam with a boiled egg on special occasions.

To Jimmy his mother had always been fat, more than twice the size of Mrs Crabb, though they were the same height.

'I think I'll get a black dress, Auntie,' said Ruby, 'black suits me, I am getting a little stout.'

'I agree, my dear,' said Aunt Alice as she poured out the tea. 'Are you going to eat now Frank dear?' she enquired politely.

Uncle Frank sniffed and took out a packet of cigarettes. 'No I'll have mine later, as it's cold meat and salad,' he replied.

'What about the potatoes?'

'I'll 'ave 'em cold,' came the reply.

'As you wish, dear,' replied Aunt Alice calmly.

'I shall wear the dress I wore to Frank's ladies evening, after all it cost enough, I think it was the most expensive dress in the shop and you know Bobbies is not cheap.'

Aunt Alice was referring to the well-known department store in Folkestone, a town some seven miles away.

'It's a lovely dress and the colour suits you,' said Ruby as she elegantly deposited half a boiled potato into her mouth.

'Mum can I be confirmed?' Jimmy's words were greeted with silence. Aunt Alice at last spoke, her brow furrowed. 'Can you what?'

'Be confirmed Aunt Alice,' replied Jimmy.

'Gordon Bennett,' gasped Aunt Alice in amazement, 'did you hear him, Ruby?'

Ruby King's mouth was still half full of potato but there was a look of incredulity on her face. She seemed lost for words.

'And what's brought this on young man?' asked Aunt Alice, looking severely at him.

Jimmy thought for a moment, unsure what to say. Suddenly he said, 'I want to be a missionary.'

Aunt Alice shook her head, causing her earrings to swing. 'Gawd's strength,' she murmured, her fork rattled against her plate as she relaxed her grip in surprise.

His mother's mouth opened like one of the roach he caught from the canal; it opened and closed again in silence.

'Pity the poor bloody natives,' commented Uncle Frank as he finished his glass of whisky.

'Can I, Mum?' persisted Jimmy.

'Er, um, well, we shall have to see.' Ruby King looked at Aunt Alice unable to make up her own mind; she invariably took her cue from her aunt.

'What is the reason for this sudden religious zeal?' Aunt Alice stared at him, her face blank.

'Er, all the boys are being confirmed Aunt Alice,' said Jimmy.

'Who are?' Aunt Alice's eyes bore into him.

'Terry Kelly, Georgie Cloke, Johnny Crabb,' replied Jimmy.

At the mention of Johnny Crabb's name Aunt Alice started. 'Good heavens above, a bright trio of beauties there, I must say, and does young Crabb want to become a missionary too by any chance?' Aunt Alice was endeavouring not to smile.

Jimmy shook his head. 'Nar Aunt Alice, I think he wants ter become a steeplejack,' replied Jimmy.

Uncle Frank started to laugh. 'I suppose he would climb the trees to look for natives for his nibs here.'

Aunt Alice and his mother were now both laughing.

'Aunt Alice, can I have my John Bull printing outfit back please?'

Aunt Alice stopped laughing and looked sternly at him. 'After what that Crabb boy did with it?' She frowned.

'I won't let him touch it ever again Aunt Alice, promise.' The urgency of his reply seemed to persuade her.'

'Alright,' she said severely, wagging her right forefinger at him. 'If I see a mark anywhere about the house or in the bars I will destroy it, do you understand?'

'Yes, Aunt Alice, I will take care of it,' said Jimmy eagerly.

'And why does young Crabb want to be a steeplejack?' asked Uncle Frank, giving Jimmy a bleary grin.

Jimmy stopped chewing and shrugged his shoulders as he replied. 'He said he'd like ter piss on people from a great height.'

'Really,' admonished his mother angrily. But for the fact Uncle Frank had doubled up laughing, Jimmy would have been in trouble.

'I don't know what to do about him Auntie,' said Ruby King, the twitch in her neck becoming suddenly pronounced.

'It's that Crabb boy,' said Aunt Alice with a sniff. 'I can well believe his reason for wishing to become a lumberjack.'

'Steeplejack, Aunt Alice,' corrected Jimmy.

'Lumberjack, steeplejack,' snapped Aunt Alice impatiently, 'that boy's a menace; he should go to confirmation classes indeed.'

Having badgered his mother into writing a note for school about attending confirmation classes and Aunt Alice into returning his printing outfit, Jimmy felt satisfied when he met Johnny Crabb on the seafront that evening.

'Got it back Crabby, and a note fer school,' said Jimmy happily.

'Good. I've gotta note too, we could get in fer this week. We'll see old Alton first thing termorrer,' replied Johnny eagerly.

The following day at mid-morning playtime, Mr Alton called Clarence Bristol to his office.

'Ah Mr Bristol, a word if you please.'

Clarence shut the office door and stood in front of the headmaster's desk, feet well apart and hands clasped behind his back, still wearing his bicycle clips.

'I've had a number of requests from parents of boys who wish to be confirmed,' began Mr Alton.

'Yes,' headmaster,' replied Clarence.

'With the boys already going, we shall have almost twenty boys going to classes; most gratifying, I'm sure you will agree?'

'Most, headmaster,' remarked Clarence drily.

'I feel sure we are making progress Mr Bristol, I know Canon Godwinson is most pleased.'

'Hm,' murmured Clarence Bristol, unimpressed.

'Crabb and King,' said Mr Alton.

'Good God,' murmured Clarence.

'Er, yes, it is surprising isn't it, but it is a fact. I have had notes from both of their mothers this morning.'

Clarence Bristol's lip curled, there must be some reason for this sudden religious urge, he was not taken in by it as Albert Charles Alton appeared to be. As he had pointed out to his long suffering wife on a number of occasions, putting Albert Alton in charge of some of the little terrors that they had was akin to employing a blind man to direct traffic.

It intrigued Clarence the more he thought about it. Later in the staff room as he drank his cup of tea his mind concentrated on it until these thoughts were swept away by the sound of a ball hitting the staff room window above his head causing him to spill some tea into his saucer.

'What the—!' he fumed as he put his cup and saucer down. He then hurried out to find the miscreant who had propelled the ball.

9

Canon Godwinson, the Rector of Hythe, took a deep breath as he stood at the top of the steps that led into Hythe parish church. The church was perched on top of a hill overlooking the town and Hythe bay was reached by a number of steps and a steep road from the centre of the town.

It was a glorious spring day. There was a faint breeze and the air was filled with the fragrance of flowers.

The verger suddenly appeared from a side door of the church and approached Canon Godwinson who was taking deep breaths of air.

'A glorious day, Mister Crispin,' smiled the Canon, a tall handsome man in his sixties.

George Crispin, the verger, did not look particularly happy. 'Good morning, Canon,' he replied.

The verger was one of those individuals who seemed to have a permanent scowl on his face, nothing was ever right for him.

'There will be six more boys for confirmation classes this evening Mr Crispin, I'll take three and Mr Catchpole the curate will take three for his class in the church hall.

'I was only saying the other day to Mr Alton that it was most gratifying, normally we have ten at most, but this year there must be almost thirty boys.' The Canon rubbed his hands together. 'Most gratifying in the midst of all our troubles, after Dunkirk and now our troubles in North Africa, we have this upsurge in religious fervour amongst our children.' He moved his head slightly, looking up into the clear blue sky. 'The Lord moves in a mysterious way does he not?'

'Yes, Canon,' sniffed George Crispin, not entirely convinced. 'They've pinched nearly all those new missionary books and those that are left have half the pages missing.'

The Canon's smile faded somewhat. 'Oh, are you sure?' he asked.

'Of course I'm sure sir,' replied the verger testily.

'Oh dear,' murmured the Canon, 'still, they were for them, as long as they read them, the seeds falling on good ground as it were,' beamed the Canon.

The verger looked at him almost in disbelief but made no comment. As far as he was concerned there was more chance of growing lettuce in Hythe high street

'Never mind Mr Crispin, I'm expecting another consignment next week. We'll only put out a few at a time, that would be the best don't you think?'

'Yes, Canon,' replied the verger in a tired voice.

That evening Johnny Crabb and Jimmy made their way up the hill to the church to attend their confirmation class. They were met in the church porch by the verger who quickly informed Johnny that he would be in the curate's class in the church hall.

'You my lad, through to the Canon's class,' he pointed at Jimmy who hurried into the church, 'and no noise,' said the verger.

After the class Jimmy made his way down the hill to the church hall, of the missionary books there had been no sign. He saw Johnny Crabb sitting on a wall outside the hall.

Johnny jumped off the wall and hurried towards him. 'Did you get any?'

'Nar,' shrugged Jimmy. 'Weren't none there, did you get any?'

'No I bloody didn't,' replied Johnny angrily, 'ain't it

bleeding choice? All evening listening ter the curate droning on and not one book, means we'll 'ave ter come again,'

'I think they are getting more in the church next week, I 'eard the Canon tell Billy Sargeant,' said Jimmy.

'Was he there too?' demanded Johnny.

Jimmy nodded in reply. 'And a lot more,' he added.

'Next week I'm coming with you, sod what the verger says,' said Johnny. 'Come on, let's go 'ome.'

Some days later Clarence Bristol, wearing his special constable's uniform, was riding his bicycle slowly down Hythe high street. It was early evening and he was making his circuit of the town before he returned to the police station. As he reached the road that led up to the church he espied the verger coming down the hill. He put on his brakes and halted just as George Crispin reached the high street.

'Evening George,' he said affably.

'Ah, hello Clarence, how are you?' replied the verger.

'Not too bad,' said Clarence, 'how are you?'

'Could be better,' said the verger.

'How are you getting on with all my boys that are in the confirmation classes?' asked Clarence quietly.

George Crispin sniffed. 'Waste of time with most of them if you ask me,' he said scowling.

'Oh,' said Clarence, raising an eyebrow.

'Aye, they've nicked all the books we had on missionary work,' said the verger.

'You do surprise me.' A leer appeared on Clarence's face. 'Anything else?'

'What do you mean?' George Crispin frowned.

'Have they taken anything else?' asked Clarence.

'Not that I know of,' came the reply, 'but I'll check,' said the verger, a worried note coming into his voice.

'I should. From what I know of some of them if it isn't

nailed down it will go, and that Crabb boy will chop up any wood that he sees, believe me,' said Clarence sternly.

The verger looked distinctly worried. He had the awful vision of a pew disappearing.

'Thank you for telling me Clarence,' he said gratefully, his thirst for a pint becoming even more acute.

'Good night George,' said Clarence as he commenced pedalling.

'Night, Clarence,' muttered a perturbed George Crispin.

On their second visit to the church for confirmation classes they were again met by the verger.

'You, down to the church hall,' he pointed at Johnny. Johnny Crabb did not move. The verger stepped forward, 'I said you, Crabb,' he growled.

'I 'eard yer. 'I'm goin to the Canon's class, my mum says I was ter,' replied Johnny.

'And I said the church hall,' snapped the verger.

'I'm stayin 'ere, my mum says so. The Canon christened me and me mum said it's 'is class I'm ter be in.' Johnny's voice was firm and clear. He was not the least overawed by the verger.

'Alright then,' replied the verger, somewhat deflated, 'but if there is any noise mind.'

They hurried off into the church and through it to a small annexe that the choir used. About twenty other boys were assembled, amongst them the Mason brothers, Smelly Potter, Ginger Baker and Luggel Pump.

Johnny and Jimmy sat at the back of the assembly and surveyed the shelves that went up to the ceiling.

'Can yer see any?' whispered Johnny.

'Dunno, what they look like?' replied Jimmy, who was cocking his ear trying to hear what the Mason brothers were saying.

'There's two on top of that cupboard,' whispered Jimmy, 'I just 'eard Micky Mason tell 'is brother.'

'Good,' muttered Johnny. 'We'll grab 'em when we can.'

Canon Godwinson came into the room beaming, his long cassock whipped up dust from the wooden floor causing one of the boys to have a fit of sneezing.

'Bless you my son,' he smiled. 'It is most gratifying to see so many of you. Let me see, two more than last week, excellent, excellent,' he rubbed his hands together with satisfaction. 'Delightful, delightful, now I'll say a few words for the benefit of the two who were not here last week.' The Canon droned on and the boys began to get restive.

'God he don't 'arf go on,' groaned Jimmy.

The Canon fortunately was a little deaf; not so Luggel Pump who suddenly started to laugh.

'It's not a laughing matter Keen, you should set an example to the younger boys,' said the Canon severely.

Luggel Pump was now half stuttering and trying not to laugh, the result being an unearthly noise, something akin to a choke.

'He's startin' ter pump now,' observed Johnny in a loud voice.

This brought laughter and a quick reaction from Luggel Pump, who swung round in his chair to strike Johnny.

'You, er, cheeky baastaad,' he stuttered.

Johnny however was too quick. He grabbed at Luggel Pump's arm and pulled at his chair which went backwards causing him to fall back and crash to the floor.

'Stop this instantly!' The Canon, his face red with anger, almost jumped out of his chair. 'You forget where you are, get back into that chair Keen and behave yourself and you too Crabb.'

'Yes, sir,' stuttered a now red-faced Luggel Pump.

At that moment the verger entered the room. 'Excuse

me, Canon, the young couple are here sir about their banns; they have an appointment.'

'Ah yes I'll see them now, Mr Crispin,' said the Canon, somewhat grateful for an excuse to dismiss the class.

'You may go now,' he said, giving Luggel Pump a severe look. 'The same time next week?' he said, giving them a weak smile as he left the room, followed by the verger.

No one moved for a moment, but the door had hardly closed when there was a mad scramble for the two missionary books. Chairs went flying and one of the books disappeared beneath a huddle of bodies.

Luggel Pump made a grab at Johnny Crabb who picked up a chair and swung it, which struck Ginger Baker first.

'Ow,' bawled Ginger as he too crashed on the heap of bodies struggling on the floor. The leg of the chair caught Luggel Pump's ear, sending him backwards.

Pandemonium now reigned. The second book suddenly came out of the scrum of boys. Jimmy made a grab at it and stuffed it in his pocket just as something hit him in the eye and he could see stars as he rolled on the floor.

Luggel Pump was now on his feet, a chair in his large hands. He swung it at Johnny who held another chair in self-defence. Unfortunately the verger chose an inopportune moment to investigate the disturbance. He rushed into the room as Luggel Pump, his back to the door, swung the chair. It struck the verger on the head just as he entered the room and he fell to the floor as if he had been poleaxed.

'Bloody 'ell Luggel yer've done it now,' said Johnny in a relieved voice.

The Canon swept into the room. As he beheld the scene there was a look of horror on his face, 'What's all this, are you all mad? Keen did you do this?'

Luggel Pump, still holding the chair began to stutter.

'He did sir,' said Smelly Potter, 'can we go sir?'

All the boys were now on their feet and the dazed verger was trying to sit up.

'Yes go, all of you, except Keen,' said the Canon angrily.

'It it it wa wa,' began Luggel Pump.

Johnny Crabb almost shot out of the door as Jimmy walked shakily out of the room, his hand to his left eye. He felt sick and was glad to get out into the fresh air.

'Yer still got that book?' asked Johnny who was waiting outside church for him.

Jimmy nodded, 'I feel bloody awful,' he moaned.

They walked slowly down the hill to the town.

'Come on, let's get a move on,' urged Johnny, 'we gotta get them coupons made straight away.'

The thought of the sweets had a soothing effect on Jimmy. He felt a little better and removed his hand from his eye.

'Cor you'll 'ave a right shiner,' said Johnny, a trifle enviously as he looked at Jimmy's eye.

This view was also expressed by Aunt Alice when he arrived at the North Star Inn. 'How did you get it, fighting I suppose?' she said impatiently.

'No Aunt Alice, I've been ter confirmation classes it 'appened there,' replied Jimmy.

'Good heavens,' she murmured in disbelief.

'What happened lad? Did you get hit by one of the natives?' asked Uncle Frank with a chuckle.

Jimmy said nothing. He was able to avoid his mother who was serving in the bar, and he hurried up to his bedroom. With the aid of his mother's scissors he cut out the index page from the missionary book. The paper was indeed identical to ration book paper and could have come from the same printers. Jimmy had traced a coupon on a piece of toilet paper and painstakingly cut up the paper. Carefully he shaded the paper with a coloured pencil and made A and D coupons with the aid of his printing outfit. The finish seemed perfect. All he had to do was to let them dry. He got into bed and in spite of his throbbing eye he was soon asleep.

The following morning Johnny Crabb and Terry Kelly were waiting for him as he left his aunt's public house.

'Did yer do 'em?' asked Johnny anxiously.

'Yep,' replied Jimmy happily.

'Cor your eyes Kingy, they're black,' gasped Terry Kelly.

'Never mind that, let's see the coupons,' said Johnny impatiently.

They walked down Stade Street and Jimmy took out the coupons and gave them to Johnny who looked at them carefully.

'They're good, bloody good,' said Johnny.

'I dun three quarters of a pound,' said Jimmy.

'Look Kelly,' said Johnny approvingly.

'Yer, they're like real,' agreed Terry with enthusiasm.

''Ere, let's go to ole Ma Howden's shop before school, and look in 'er winder,' said Johnny.

'Yer, good idea,' agreed Jimmy.

'I've got nine pence halfpenny, 'ow much 'ave you got Crabby?'

'Two and six,' replied Johnny proudly.

'I got six pence halfpenny,' said Terry.

They started to run towards Mrs Howden's shop which was situated in Prince Albert Road, in the middle of a row of terraced houses. The shop window was simply decorated with cardboard dummies, the pride of place being taken by a row of large jars running the full length of the window, with a backdrop consisting of a green curtain on a runner. The jars contained boiled sweets of every description, toffees, liquorice allsorts, winegums, everything to tempt and please hungry boys.

They ran down Prince Albert Road and arrived panting

outside the shop. It was closed, the sign on the door made that clear, but this was not noticed by the boys as they gazed dumbfounded in the window. A disaster had happened. The jars were all empty, with the exception of one in the centre and all it contained was a few dolly mixtures which looked as if they were stuck together.

'She got no bloody sweets,' puffed Jimmy.

'Ain't it bleedin choice,' gasped Johnny.

'Just a few mouldy dolly mixtures.'

At that moment the green curtain was pulled aside and Mrs Howden's face appeared.

'Aw, Jesus,' groaned Terry Kelly,' she's got 'er glasses back.'

'That's bleedin shit it,' said Johnny angrily, 'after all we've been through.'

Mrs Howden began shaking her fist at them and waving them away.

'What's up wiv 'er the old kite,' said Jimmy.

Johnny made a face at her and then spoke, 'Come on we'd better get on or we'll be late.'

They started to trot down the road in the direction of school.

'I bet Clokey and his gang 'ave 'ad all them sweets,' puffed Terry.

'Yeah,' agreed Johnny, 'greedy pigs.'

They arrived at school just as the assembly bell rang and further discussion was impossible, having settled in their classes and the school register called, the daily uphill task of imparting knowledge began.

At play time they realised something was up. Ginger Baker had told them that the Clokes and Collins were in Mr Alton's office.

'I saw a copper come with Ma Howden too,' said Ginger, 'and old bang bang Godwinson's here,' added Smelly Potter.

It quickly dawned on them that the scheme with the sweet coupons had run its course and that trouble was brewing.

'After all my bloody work,' groaned Johnny.

'*Your* work,' protested Jimmy. 'Mine you mean, I made 'em.'

'I went to them two confirmation classes didn't I?' said Johnny, his voice rising.

'And so did I, look at my bleeding eyes, my uncle said I looked like a panda this morning,' replied Jimmy dolefully.

'I saw ole potato crisp the verger this morning,' grinned Ginger Baker. 'Got a plaster on his 'ead, looks like he's got a lump on it the size of an egg.'

'Ha ha ha ha,' laughed Johnny, 'old Luggel give 'im a right crack on the nut wiv a chair.'

'Who hit you Kingy?' asked Ginger Baker.

'Don't bloody know. I think it was Billy Mason's boot, but I don't remember much about it,' replied Jimmy.

The bell rang and they trooped unwillingly back to class. Clarence Bristol stood in front of the class his feet apart, arms behind his back, with his bicycle clips keeping his neatly creased grey flannels tight to his legs. He looked like a bird of prey waiting to pounce.

He peered over his glasses, then spoke in a quiet sinister voice. 'Every boy stand up that has been going to confirmation classes.'

Johnny, Jimmy and Terry Kelly got reluctantly to their feet, as did Ginger Baker, Smelly Potter and Johnny Green.

'You can sit down Kelly, this does not concern you,' snapped Clarence. Terry Kelly quickly sat down.

'At the moment in the assembly hall the headmaster, Inspector Hall and Canon Godwinson are questioning the Clokes, Collins, Jamison, Sullivan, Saltwood, the Masons and Davis concerning the riot that took place at confirmation class yesterday evening and more seriously a fraud that has been taking place over counterfeit sweet coupons at Mrs Howden's establishment. I shall question you before the headmaster and inspector and I want the truth, Crabb do you hear?'

'Yes, sir,' replied Johnny.

'The truth Crabb,' said Clarence his voice rising.

'Yes sir, but I ain't been in old Ma Howden's shop,' protested Johnny, 'fer weeks sir thats the truth.'

'We'll soon find out won't we?' said Clarence grimly. 'Which of you *has* been in Mrs Howden's shop during the past week?'

There was a hush in the class, those seated scarcely breathed less they attracted Clarence Bristol's attention.

'None of you?' leered Clarence.

'I went in with my mum, sir,' said a weak voiced Smelly Potter.

Clarence nodded, but made no comment. Then he looked at Jimmy.

'And last night's riot, what have you got to say about it King?'

'Nuffin, sir,' replied Jimmy.

'Nothing boy,' roared Clarence, 'you have nothing to say?'

'No, sir,' said an unrepentant Jimmy. 'Don't remember anything about it after Luggel Pump swung that chair and cracked the verger on the nut.'

'And what happened then?' growled Clarence.

'Somefin' 'it me sir, I don't remember any more until Crabby helped me out of the door. I felt sick, sir.'

'Yes I 'elped 'im sir, he couldn't stand up. Luggel Pump went barmy with that chair, nearly 'it me sir,' said Johnny.

'Indeed.' Clarence Bristol's face changed slightly. He knew from past experience that he would make little progress, far better to let his superiors pit their wits against them, perhaps he would then be appreciated a little more.

'The rest of the class will take out their arithmetic books and do the questions I have set on the blackboard. You boys standing follow me, and if there is any noise in here I will come back and cane all of you.'

He led the way out of the classroom and down the corridor to the hall. A dozen boys were already there as were Mr Alton, Inspector Hall, Canon Godwinson and the redoubtable Mrs Howden.

'Stand in line facing the rostrum,' snapped Clarence who stood next to them at the end of the line.

Inspector Hall spoke with the full authority his position gave him in the town. He puffed out his chest and looked around. 'Since this is a most serious matter headmaster, Canon, I will begin the questioning of these boys.'

Both the headmaster and the Canon nodded their agreement. The inspector stepped up onto the rostrum, his eyes narrowed as he looked down at Johnny and Jimmy.

'First I will ask Mrs Howden if she would kindly identify any of these boys – Mrs Howden, please step this way.'

Ivy Howden walked slowly down the line then stopped.

'This one come in the other day with his mother,' she said pointing at Smelly Potter.

'Did he tender forged sweet coupons?' asked the inspector.

'No his mother bought some chocolate biscuits with her ration book,' replied Mrs Howden.

'Then we are not concerned with him,' said the inspector tersely.

She stopped in front of Johnny Crabb, uncertainly.

'I ain't been in your shop,' said Johnny quickly. 'My mum told me not to, said you've got mice.'

'Mice,' croaked Mrs Howden, her face going red. 'That's a lie, that's a libel, you heard that,' she looked around.

'We are not concerned about that,' snapped the inspector.

'Well I am,' retorted Ivy Howden, glaring at him. The headmaster and Clarence exchanged a glance. It was as Clarence expected; the inspector was not getting very far.

'Can we get on Mrs Howden please,' said the inspector, his tone softening.

Mrs Howden carried on along the line until she reached the end.

'No, none of these boys in the last ten days,' she said.

'Good. Now I'll question these boys about their motives for going to confirmation classes and the reasons for being there, there seems to be a definite connection.' The inspector looked about importantly as if he had solved a major crime.

'You, boy,' the inspector's leather-gloved hand pointed at Jimmy. 'You received those black eyes at confirmation classes I understand. How did it happen?'

All eyes were now on Jimmy who stood with his legs apart, hands behind his back, much as he had seen Clarence stand.

'Dunno, sir,' replied Jimmy shortly.

'You don't know,' repeated the inspector frowning.

'No sir, I don't remember much after Luggel Pump 'it the verger on the nut wiv a chair.'

Mr Alton and Clarence exchanged glances and Canon Godwinson looked uncomfortable as he peered at Jimmy.

'I see. He struck you too then?' said the inspector.

'I don't know sir, somefing 'it me, my mum says I'm not ter go ter confirmation classes again and my Uncle Frank says I look like a bleedin' panda.'

'King, I shall cane you if you use such language again,' said the headmaster angrily. The inspector put his gloved hand in front of his mouth but made no comment. At last he spoke, deciding on a different ploy and not realising the formidability of his opponent.

'And why did you go to confirmation classes in the first place?' The inspector leaned forward expectantly and both Mr Alton and the Canon stared hard at Jimmy.

'Cos I want ter be a missionary sir,' replied Jimmy, his face devoid of expression.

The headmaster started to blink as a leer appeared on Clarence Bristol's face. The Canon frowned while the inspector put a gloved hand in front of his face as he spoke again.

'A missionary eh boy?' said the inspector.

Mr Alton's tongue seemed to be pushing into his cheek in an effort to keep his face straight, whilst Clarence Bristol was looking down at his shoes.

'Yes sir, and my Uncle Frank said if that is what 'appens to yer at confirmation classes he's glad he's a heathen.'

'Really,' snapped Canon Godwinson, as the inspector suddenly turned and faced the other way. The headmaster was now looking at his shoes and Clarence at the hall ceiling.

The inspector abruptly turned to face Jimmy again. 'So you do not know how all the commotion started laddie?'

'No, sir,' replied Jimmy.

'And you boy,' the inspector pointed at Johnny. 'You tell me quick now,' he said sharply.

If the inspector had expected to intimidate Johnny he was soon to be disappointed.

'It was Luggel Pump wiv a chair, he swung it and clocked the verger.'

'That's enough Crabb,' said the headmaster tersely. 'What else happened?'

'He went potty, sir. Since he's been at the post office he's gorn all funny like,' said Johnny.

'Post office,' repeated the headmaster curiously. 'Luggel, er, I mean Keen, at the post office?' he frowned.

'Yes headmaster,' cut in Canon Godwinson, 'I used my er hem influence and spoke in his favour with the postal authorities which I am beginning to regret.' The Canon shook his head.

'What does he do there?' asked the headmaster.

'A sorter I think,' replied the Canon.

'Good gracious,' murmured Mr Alton. 'Was that wise Canon?'

'Wise! They need sorters, there is a war on you know.' The headmaster pursed his lips but did not reply.

'Luggel can't read, sir, he's still got a Chicken Lickin book at home and he can't read that,' piped up Johnny with a grin.

'My goodness,' the Canon's face seemed to register bewilderment.

'I don't suppose it matters,' remarked Clarence drily. 'Postmaster's not worried as long as all the letters and parcels are cleared each evening, where they go to doesn't worry him.'

'I would hardly think that is the mandate he is given by the Postmaster General,' snapped Canon Godwinson angrily.

'Perhaps not, Canon, but it's the principle by which the postmaster seems to operate,' retorted Clarence, who had not liked the Canon ever since he had been passed over for the headmastership when Albert Alton was appointed.

The inspector shook his head, he seemed to have lost all control of the interrogation.

'Maybe that's why that parcel I sent to my sister never arrived,' remarked Ivy Howden.

'Look, I'm not concerned about the post office,' the inspector's voice rose. 'I want to know what happened at this confirmation class, you tell me,' the inspector pointed at Ginger Baker.

Ginger shrugged. 'The chairs fell over as they scrambled to get the two missionary books.'

'Ah,' the inspector said quietly, 'go on, and?'

'There was a pile of boys on the floor after the books,' replied Ginger.

'Presumably they did not all wish to be missionaries!' said the inspector sarcastically.

'Don't think so, sir,' said Ginger.

'Why then?' snapped the inspector.

'To get the paper out of them, sir,' replied Ginger.

'In order to make illegal sweet coupons?' said the inspector triumphantly.

'Don't know, sir,' replied Ginger.

The inspector looked at Mr Alton and then at the unhappy Canon who as chairman of the school governors would have the unpleasant task of informing the rest of the governors of the unfortunate sequence of events.

'I'm sure that there is now no doubt of what happened and why it happened and I think the answer is for the boys concerned to make it up to Mrs Howden from their own sweet coupon allowance, with the assistance of their parents to see that the coupons are handed over during the months to come.'

This suggestion received immediate nods of approval from both the headmaster and Canon Godwinson, though Clarence Bristol did not seem to hear as he balanced on the balls of his feet, hands clasped behind his back, looking up at the ceiling. His posture was now being copied by Johnny Crabb, then Jimmy King and Ginger Baker adopted the same stance. If it passed unnoticed by the headmaster and the Canon, it certainly did not by the inspector whose mouth was doing contortions in an effort not to laugh.

'I think I'll leave now headmaster, Canon,' he said quickly, 'I think I can leave the matter in yours and Mr Bristol's capable hands, may I escort you home Mrs Howden?' he smiled.

'Er, thank you inspector,' replied Ivy Howden quickly, flattered by such attention.

Immediate punishment was administered by Clarence Bristol whilst the headmaster and Canon Godwinson retired to the former's office for a cup of tea.

For once Johnny and Jimmy escaped a caning and swaggered back to their classroom. The class looked up as they entered.

'Pudden, he's goin ter cane you when he comes back he could hear you in the hall.'

'I wasn't,' protested Mavis Pullen, her face now going red.

'He 'eard you and pisspot Chambers,' said Johnny.

'You are rude Crabb,' said the pretty dark haired Doreen Chambers who sat next to Mavis.

'I wasn't was I?' Mavis looked around for support.

'Don't believe him,' said Doreen with a sniff.

'Alright, you see then,' said Johnny. 'Didn't 'e Kingy, you 'eard im?'

'Yeah he did,' nodded Jimmy. 'He did he said I'm goin' ter cane their bums when I get back for talking.'

'You are rude, King,' hissed Mavis.

'He's a bigger liar than Crabb,' said Doreen with a shake of her auburn curls.

'Ha ha ha,' laughed Johnny and Jimmy as they returned to their desks.

'What 'appened?' asked Terry Kelly eagerly.

'Clokey and 'is gang are getting six of the best and they've lost their sweet ration for three months,' said Johnny with some satisfaction.

'Serves them bloody right, all she 'ad left were a few mouldy dolly mixtures,' sniffed Jimmy miserably.

'Anyway I can't see them handin' over their sweet coupons.'

'I bet they don't,' agreed Terry Kelly.

This view was also expressed by a perspiring Clarence who, having administered the punishments, joined the headmaster in his office. The Canon had departed and the headmaster poured Clarence a lukewarm cup of tea.

'Canon Godwinson is very perturbed about this whole unfortunate business Mr Bristol, his hopes of a record number of confirmees seem about to be dashed,' sighed the headmaster.

Clarence stood, cup and saucer in hand, opposite the headmaster's desk. He looked over his glasses.

'Oh!' he remarked disinterestedly.

'Yes, he feels that the classes will be poorly attended.'

'We can make sure that they are well attended,' said Clarence as he sipped his tea.

'How?' queried Mr Alton.

'By caning any boy who does not attend,' said Clarence as he stirred his tea again.

'Well I hardly think we can do that you know, after all it is after school hours.'

'It's up to you headmaster,' said Clarence icily.

'Er, yes, I will give it some thought,' Mr Alton hesitated. 'As for this coupon business your inspector did find a way out,' the headmaster sounded a little happier.

Clarence put his cup and saucer down on the desk none too gently, and the spoon fell onto the desk. As he put it back in the saucer he remarked sarcastically, 'The inspector is as gullible as Canon Godwinson. He has as much chance of getting those sweet coupons as the Canon has of walking to France. If you will excuse me headmaster, I'll get back to my class.'

Without another word Clarence turned and left the office leaving the headmaster his lips pursed scratching at his scalp.

On the morning of the next confirmation class, Clarence made it clear to the class that they were expected to be at confirmation class that evening.

'And if any boy is not there from my class I shall cane him,' he hissed, looking around the class.

'But sir it's out of school time,' protested Johnny Crabb, standing up.

'Don't argue with me Crabb or I'll cane you now.' Johnny could see that Clarence meant it so he wisely sat down, though later he gave vent to his feelings.

'It's a bloody swiz,' he howled, surrounded by his pals in the playground.

Jimmy and Ginger Baker quickly nodded their agreement.

'Bleedin' liberty if yer ask me,' said Jimmy. 'Me mum won't give me a note saying not ter go, I asked 'er but she won't,' he said miserably.

'Nor mine,' groaned Johnny.

At dinner time he went home with his sisters. His mother had some mackerel and when she had cooked it sat engrossed in an old magazine as the children ate it. Johnny picked it up as she served out the pudding. What had interested her was the story of a murder that had taken place some years previously in London. The murderer had buried his wife in their garden and it had only been discovered when a bone had been dug up by a dog. Then the whole garden was dug up by the police.

'You shouldn't read that Johnny, it's not for you,' admonished his mother, taking the magazine from him. 'You eat your pudding,' she smiled.

Johnny tucked into his pudding and forgot about it, until he arrived that evening for confirmation class.

They had arrived early and wandered down to the crypt for something to do and as the door was unlocked they were able to browse around it.

The crypt housed a large quantity of human bones that had been put there when the cemetery had been modified. They looked at the piles of femurs, tibias and skulls.

'That one looks a bit like ole Clarence,' said Jimmy, pointing at a scull.

'Um,' agreed Johnny deep in thought.

'We'd better go back or we'll be late,' said Jimmy.

'Yeah, you go back, I'll foller, I'm goin ter 'ave a pee first,' replied Johnny.

'Alright,' said Jimmy, running back up the stone stairs.

Johnny swiftly picked up two skulls, two femurs and two tibias, he then crept back up the stairs making sure he was unobserved. He then hid them in some bushes adjacent to the choir annex, just as he observed the verger approaching and about to lock up the crypt.

Quickly he returned to the church as the verger locked the crypt door. He smiled as he hurried into the room, the scene of the first confirmation class.

The Canon beamed at the full class. With the exception of Luggel Pump every boy was there. It was most gratifying to him and he was prepared to forgive and forget in the true Christian spirit and start afresh, unaware of the debt he undoubtedly owed to Clarence Bristol.

Outside school and the special constabulary Clarence Bristol's interest was his garden and in particular his front garden which was much larger than his back garden due to the particular shape of the plot of land on which his house was built. Every evening he spent a little time on it, clipping the edges of the lawns which would have been a credit to any bowling green. The hedge was perfect, such precision was only seen in ornamental gardens or the grounds of stately homes. His rose beds accommodated a fine collection of hybrid tea roses and were admired by passers by much to Clarence's infinite joy. That evening as he hoed the few uninvited weeds he would have been horrified if he had known what his adversary Johnny Crabb was hatching in his mind.

After confirmation class that evening Johnny

accompanied Jimmy to his aunt's public house. Outside the saloon bar door they stopped and began to talk.

'Yer can't come in Crabby, she won't let yer,' said Jimmy.

'Can yer get me a large paper bag,' replied Johnny, unperturbed.

'What for?'

'Never mind wot for, go and get,' snapped Johnny.

Jimmy shrugged and disappeared through the side door of the pub. Moments later he reappeared holding a large brown carrier bag.

"Ere yar,' he said, handing it to Johnny.

'Thanks, mate,' said Johnny, grabbing it and running back the way they had come and in the direction of the church.

Jimmy frowned again, what was he up to, he wondered. He was running in the opposite direction to his home.

He could hear his aunt calling him from the kitchen.

'Yes Aunt Alice,' he replied; it was getting dark and he was glad to return to the warm and smoky atmosphere of the North Star Inn.

10

It was some weeks later that the first bones appeared in Clarence's front garden. After a heavy rain storm the top of a skull appeared through the earth in one of the borders. The discovery was made by Clarence's son Wilfred who was home on leave from the army. Wilfred, who was a corporal in the Royal Military Police, was much like his father in looks and manner.

'You'll have to report it Dad,' said Wilfred as they examined the skull in the front garden.

'I am well aware of my duty my son,' replied his father coolly. Clarence picked up a rake that he had been using and proceeded to rake the area where the skull had been. Suddenly he pulled up another bone.

'My God, Dad, that's a leg bone,' gasped Wilfred.

Beads of perspiration began to appear on Clarence's forehead and the rake trembled in his hands.

'I'd better report this straight away. I cannot understand this,' he muttered.

He went into the house and made a telephone call. Within minutes a car drew up outside and two men got out.

Clarence and his son were still in the garden. By this time they had found a second skull.

'Detective Inspector White of Folkestone CID,' the man said, taking out his identification wallet and holding it in front of a now visibly shaken Clarence.

'Er, yes, inspector,' mumbled Clarence, 'come in.' He held the gate open for the men to enter.

'Sergeant Tyson from my department,' said the inspector as he strode into the garden. 'And you say you found them here? Just below the surface?' said the inspector pointing to a neat border.

'Er, yes inspector,' mumbled Clarence.

'I was with my father when we saw the first skull poking through the earth,' said Wilfred Bristol.

The inspector looked at one of the bleached femurs, a flicker of a smile appeared on his face and then he turned to Clarence.

'Mr Bristol I would not be positive but I'd say this bone has been in your garden only recently, it's too white and there is no discolouration. I'll let our forensic experts look at it of course and I'll send men to dig up your garden but I think I am right, so do not touch anything until my men arrive.'

'Er, no,' stuttered Clarence.

'May I use your telephone please?'

'Y-yes,' replied Clarence.

'Sergeant, put these bones in the car,' said the inspector.

'Yes, sir.

'Mr Bristol, I understand you are a special constable, so I will put you in charge of the garden until further men arrive.'

'Yes inspector, I'll go and put on my uniform,' said Clarence.

The inspector made his phone call and returned to the garden where his sergeant was talking to Wilfred Bristol.

'My father is always forking over these borders inspector, I'm surprised nothing was discovered before this.'

'So am I, but in view of the fact that they are human bones there are procedures that have to be followed.'

At this point Clarence emerged from the house wearing his uniform, complete with his peaked hat.

'Constable Bristol,' began the inspector, 'nothing must

be touched until my men arrive and I understand the senior officer here in Hythe will be here soon. I am taking these bones back to Folkestone for examination. When your senior local officer arrives I would suggest that you find out if any bones have gone missing, you understand?'

Suddenly it dawned on Clarence. He swallowed hard as he realised that it could all be a practical joke.

'The crypt,' he muttered.

'Exactly, Constable Bristol,' said the inspector, who had been brought up in the town and was aware of the crypt at Hythe parish church.

'Why I'll—' Clarence spluttered with subdued rage.

When the two detectives had departed with the bones, Clarence, his face white with anger, took his bicycle from its shed behind the house and put on his bicycle clips.

'Going out, Dad? asked Wilfred as his father pushed the bicycle out of the front gate.

Clarence did not hear him as he mounted the bicycle and then pedalled furiously down the road, his head over the handlebars. Wilfred Bristol shrugged and then took a packet of cigarettes from his tunic breast pocket and methodically lit one. Suddenly he started to smile, then he burst out laughing, that was it! One of his father's boys had nicked some bones from the crypt and put them in the garden.

Wilfred leaned on the gate and rocked with laughter as his father, still pedalling hard, approached the church. By a fortunate coincidence he met the verger outside the crypt.

'Do you know how many bones you should have?' asked a panting Clarence Bristol.

The verger looked at Clarence Bristol as if he had just sprouted wings.

'How many? What are you on about, are you alright?'

'In the crypt man,' snapped Clarence angrily.

'There's no need to take that tone with me Mr Bristol,' said the verger haughtily.

Clarence modified his voice. 'Do you know what bones you have in the crypt?' he said quietly, emphasising each word as he did so.

'Yes of course, there is a record from when they were removed from the old graveyard. They were all recorded in the parish register and each bone was counted and checked against burial records so we know exactly how many we have.'

'Well I think you are going to have to count them all again,' said Clarence drily.

'What!' gasped the verger, his face reddening.

'I think some have turned up in my front garden Mr Crispin, the police have them now and forensic department at Ashford will be examining them shortly, and it will save a lot of time and trouble if you could check your bones and tell me if any are missing.'

'What! count them? Have you seen how many there are?'

Clarence Bristol shook his head then put his bicycle against the church wall.

'Come, I'll show you,' said the verger as he led the way to the crypt steps. 'I'll put on the light,' he said, going down the stone stairs to the crypt door.

Clarence followed him down the steps. He knew that there were some bones stored there but was not prepared for the amount.

'Look,' said the verger.

The crypt, lit by a cobweb-covered forty-watt bulb, was filled with stacks of human bones of every description. Skulls were placed on shelves and heaped on top of each other whilst femurs and tibias were in orderly heaps on the floor.

'Good heavens,' muttered Clarence.

'Exactly,' replied the verger. 'It would take me days to count that lot.'

'Even so, it will have to be done, but that's not my decision, I'll inform Canon Godwinson and let him decide,' said Clarence.

The verger sniffed angrily. 'If there's any missing it's those boys we had for confirmation classes.' He gingerly felt the spot where the chair had struck him.

'You could well be right Mr Crispin,' said Clarence in his formal manner, 'but we will have to find out,' he added grimly.

The Canon listened intently as Clarence informed him of his suspicions in regard to the bones found in his garden.

'Its only supposition at this stage Canon, but there is some foundation to it,' explained Clarence as he stood in the spacious hall of the vicarage.

The Canon nodded. 'Yees,' he said slowly, 'but highly possible.' He made a clicking noise with his tongue as he meditated. 'How annoying, but we have an obligation to the deceased, two sculls did you say Mr Bristol?'

'Yes, sir,' replied Clarence.

'Then the verger and the curate must count ours immediately, that will give us some indication if they belong here,' said the Canon firmly.

'Thank you, sir,' replied Clarence. 'I am on duty at the police station at 6.30 Canon, if you would be so good as to inform me there it could save a lot of police time and we would be grateful.'

'I certainly will Mr Bristol,' said the Canon as he opened the heavy oak front door of the vicarage.

'Thank you, Canon,' replied Clarence as he stepped outside into the porch and put on his hat.

'Not at all,' said the Canon, firmly closing the door.

As Clarence mounted his bicycle he could see the outline of the Canon through the coloured panes of the vicarage front door, giving the verger instructions.

'Sooner him than me,' muttered Clarence as he pedalled out of the vicarage drive and turned to go down the hill to the town. He smiled grimly as he put his mind to the possible perpetrator of this practical joke, if indeed it was. Clarence felt suddenly chilled as he mulled on the alternative to a joke. With this thought in mind he returned home to find four men digging up his front garden. His son met him at the front gate with the words, 'They've found more bones Dad, and Mum has gone to stay with Aunt Rita at Lydd until its all over. We'll have to get our own tea.' Clarence ignored his son as one of the men put a large boot on one of his prize roses.

'Watch where you are putting your big feet,' he said angrily.

The man ignored him as he pushed his spade into the lawn almost with relish and began digging it up.

By nine that evening a tired and dusty verger accompanied by an equally ill-humoured curate informed the Canon that there were indeed two skulls missing from the crypt.

The Canon immediately informed the police station duty sergeant.

'Thank you Canon, and you will be checking the rest of the remains?' asked the sergeant politely.

'Yes, in due course,' came the reply.

When Clarence returned to the station prior to booking out, the sergeant informed him of the Canon's message. There were grins from the regular policemen when the sergeant remarked that all the bones in the crypt would have to be counted as well.

'Perhaps some of your boys would like to help count them,' he said, glancing at a constable who did not like Clarence.

This brought forth a burst of laughter which subsided as he retorted icily, 'At least I do know that they can count,' he said, looking about him before he signed the station book and stalked out.

As Clarence pedalled slowly home that night he resolved to find the culprit, but this he never managed to do. Johnny Crabb was his prime suspect but he was unable to get him to admit it; his questions were met by denials and a blank expression.

Clarence finally gave up, having decided it was better to let the matter rest than make himself look even more foolish by pursuing what seemed to be a fruitless task.

Johnny Crabb, in his relentless duel with Clarence, had won a round. The only person to share his secret was Jimmy King, who summed up their feelings by saying loudly, 'Serve the ole bastard right.'

'Yeah,' agreed Johnny as they howled with laughter.

11

It was Saturday afternoon and Jimmy stood outside the Grove cinema. His great aunt Alice had given him the complimentary ticket she received for hanging up the Grove cinema's poster in one of her bars.

The films showing were both A certificate, which meant that Jimmy had to be accompanied by an adult and so far every adult he had approached had refused to take him in.

He looked disconsolately at the pictures in the glass cases of next week's film and the posters on the wall in the foyer. Then he noticed three figures approaching. His mouth opened in astonishment. They were all in flying gear, sheepskin-lined boots and jacket and leather trousers, and they sounded like Americans.

Jimmy approached them and looked up at the middle one, a broad-shouldered man with a crew cut. He held up his ticket.

'Will yer take me in mister?' he asked.

'Take you in son?' drawled the American.

'Do what kid?' said the second American.

'Yeah I must be accompanied by an adult, it's an A film.'

'Sure,' grinned the first American. 'Come on, kid.'

'Here's my ticket,' said Jimmy.

'Keep it,' son,' said the first American bending down and looking into the pay box.

'Say gorgeous, three tickets and the boy here,' he said, putting a pound note down on the brass ticket counter.

The woman in the pay box preened herself and dispensed the tickets, unused to such flattery.

'Come on, kid,' grinned the American and Jimmy, pleased as Punch, followed them into the cinema.

It was the interval and the Americans bought ice cream, giving one to Jimmy.

'What's your name, son?' asked the first American.

'Jimmy, er I mean Jimmy King,' he replied. 'What's yours?'

The first American grinned. 'I'm Chick, this is Hank next to me and on the end seat eyeing the ticket girl is Bud.'

'What yer doin' here?' asked Jimmy as he spooned up a lump of ice cream from the tub he was holding.

Chick grinned. 'We baled out this morning on our way back from a raid, our plane crashed in the sea. Lucky for us the wind blew us towards the land or we would have been wet. We got hit and couldn't make it back to base, we're waiting for a truck to come and take us back to base. We've been at your police precinct house.'

Jimmy frowned, 'Oh the police station you mean.'

'Yep that's right,' grinned Chick.

'Where do you come from Chick?'

'Wyoming,' he replied.

'Cor,' gasped Jimmy, 'are there cowboys there?'

'Sure, plenty,' replied Chick.

''Ave yer seen Roy Rogers?'

Chick began to laugh. 'Nope, Jimmy, never.'

'Oh,' replied Jimmy, a little disappointed. 'Do yer live on a ranch Chick?' asked Jimmy hopefully.

The American shook his head and then spoke quietly, 'Nope, I was brought up in an orphanage, then I went straight into the army air corps.'

Jimmy's face dropped as he said quietly, 'You had no mum and dad Chick.'

'Nope. Where's your dad Jimmy?' asked Chick suddenly.

'In the navy on a cruiser,' replied Jimmy proudly. His face suddenly clouded as he thought of his father. 'Me mum says he's gone so's his ship she said she 'ad a letter, I don't believe her Chick, he promised me he did he's comin' 'ome.'

Jimmy's eyes misted and the Americans exchanged glances.

'Sure he is Jimmy,' smiled Chick.

'Too right he is son,' grinned Hank.

'Sure he is kid,' said Bud, winking at him.

Jimmy nodded and blinked his eyes. The dim lights spared him any further embarrassment and the programme began.

Later, when Jimmy proudly left the cinema with his American friends, Chick spoke to him.

'Which way to the police precinct house, Jimmy?'

Jimmy grinned. 'Police station. I'll show yer Chick, this way.'

Outside the little police station Jimmy stopped. 'This is it Chick, he said sadly.

The American airman looked down at him. 'Bye son,' he said kindly. He put a hand inside his flying jacket and took out a full packet of chewing gum.

'Here,' he said, giving it to Jimmy, 'thought I had a pack left somewhere.' He smiled.

Jimmy's face lit up. 'Cor lummy,' he gasped, 'thanks Chick, I might see yer again?'

'Think not, son,' the American shook his head. 'Lightning doesn't strike in the same place,' he grinned, 'hope you see your pa soon Jimmy.'

'Bye, Chick,' mumbled Jimmy.

'Cheerio, old buddy,' grinned Hank.

'Bye, Hank,' sniffed Jimmy.

'See yer, son,' said Bud, giving him a wink.

'Bye, Bud,' replied Jimmy sadly.

The three Americans went into the little police station, leaving Jimmy standing forlornly outside on the pavement. Suddenly an idea seemed to strike Jimmy. His face changed and he ran back down the road.

That evening he called at Johnny Crabb's home.

'Look,' he said proudly.

'Where d'yer get it?' said Johnny, looking at the flare parachute.

'I swopped it with Clokey for a packet of American chewing gum,' replied Jimmy.

Quickly Jimmy explained about his meeting with the American airmen outside the Grove cinema.

'Look, I've still got my ticket, you can see the last showing if yer want to.'

'Can I?' said Johnny.

'Sure, here,' Jimmy gave him the ticket.

'I will then,' grinned Johnny. 'Come on then Kingy, let's try your parachute first.'

12

Since the incident with the wheelbarrow, Mr Turner the caretaker looked for every chance to get Johnny Crabb into trouble. In all fairness he did not have to look very hard as Johnny would always meet trouble more than halfway.

On one particular Monday morning at assembly, the headmaster, looking very stern, announced that he had received a complaint from a lady living close to the school.

'This lady says a boy from this school threw a stone and broke her front room window, I want the culprit to own up now.' He paused but there was no movement in the hall. Then he looked in the direction of Clarence Bristol's class and an expectant hush fell on the hall.

'Very well, I will make my own enquiries and woe betide the culprit when I find out who it is.'

He exchanged glances with Clarence Bristol and they both looked in the direction of Johnny Crabb, Jimmy King and Terry Kelly, who were standing next to each other.

'Now, my next announcement concerns a visit to the cinema,' continued Mr Alton. His words caused a subdued murmur until Clarence Bristol's voice rang out. 'Quiet, or there will be detentions.'

The murmur subsided and the headmaster continued. 'Thanks to the generosity of the American Red Cross the whole school is going to the Grove cinema on Wednesday afternoon to see a film called *The Drum*.

'Cor,' muttered Jimmy, 'Sabu's in it Crabby.'

'Are you talking King?' barked Clarence Bristol.
'I was telling Crabby who was in it, sir,' explained Jimmy.
'Detention on the line after school,' replied Clarence.
'Yes, sir,' replied Jimmy, a little crestfallen.
'That is all,' said Mr Alton. 'Now file quietly to your classes.'

Jimmy did not know how Johnny Crabb came to be blamed for the broken window, but on the morning of the visit to the cinema Johnny was caned before the whole school and told that he would stay in school instead of going to the cinema that afternoon. Jimmy knew it wasn't Johnny who had broken the window as they had both been fishing when the damage occurred. When he told Clarence Bristol of the fact his reply had been terse. 'If you come to me with any more yarns like that, King, I will cane you.'

He had told his mother, but she was not interested. His Aunt Alice and Uncle Frank had ignored him.

Although he had strenuously denied responsibility, Johnny was caned. Jimmy could see his two young sisters in Mrs Woollet's class both crying silently as the strokes landed.

'It was ole turnip 'ead who told on me, it was 'is nephew from Folkestone who did it, the grammer grub, 'e 'ad a catapult.'

'Did he?' queried Jimmy.

'Clokey saw 'im that day outside the school, Clokey told ole Bristol and 'e told 'im ter clear off,' said Johnny bitterly.

'Told me too, said he'd cane me as well,' said Jimmy with feeling.

'I'll get 'im,' said Johnny grimly, 'you see if I don't.'

Jimmy had asked his aunt for the Grove complimentary ticket and she had given it to him as always. Perhaps she looked on it as an investment for a quiet life with Jimmy out of the way for three hours.

'I don't want ter see the rotten ole film,' sniffed Johnny.

Later after school dinner Jimmy produced the ticket, ''Ere Crabby, you can 'ave my complimentary and go later,' said Jimmy holding out the ticket.

'Yer mean it?' said Johnny his eyes misty.

'Yer take it,' replied Jimmy.

Johnny put the ticket into his pocket as the bell rang for classes and they went into school.

Jimmy knew that Johnny Crabb had a fascination for locks and keys, of which he had acquired a considerable number, in fact his bunch of keys would have done credit to the chief yeoman warder of the Tower of London.

Jimmy thought nothing of it on the day of the school's visit to the cinema. Clarence Bristol had set Johnny four arithmetic questions which Jimmy immediately did for him as he was good at maths, before the school lined up in the playground. Jimmy enjoyed the film which was about the North West Frontier of India and he forgot all about Johnny Crabb.

After the film the children were sent home and Clarence Bristol returned to school to dismiss Johnny Crabb.

Much to his surprise Crabb was still there and the sums were correct.

'You may go Crabb,' he said curtly.

Johnny did not reply but hurried out of school and ran out of the playground and into the road in the direction of his home. Clarence Bristol collected his bicycle and left just after, noticing that the caretaker was working in his shed. This had also been observed by Johnny Crabb and also the fact that the open lock had been left hanging on the staple. Johnny doubled down a side street and then came back behind the caretaker's shed. Having watched Clarence Bristol depart he crept round the shed and silently slipped the lock over the hasp. Snap, he closed the lock and the caretaker, listening to a wireless as he worked, was quite unaware of what happened. Johnny then ran home while Mr Turner carried on repairing the school's gardening equipment.

His wife had gone to see her sister at Ashford and had left him a cold tea in the kitchen. Later he looked at his watch. 'Five o'clock,' he muttered, straightening his back. 'I'll put the kettle on,' he said as he tried to open the door.

It was not until 9.15 that a passer by heard his shouts and banging and informed the police.

The station sergeant smiled as he put down the phone. 'Constable Bristol,' he said slowly, 'one for you.'

Clarence Bristol, who was on late turn and who had just reported for duty, looked sourly at him.

'Someone's got locked in the caretaker's shed at your school. Go and investigate the matter please.'

Clarence nodded and left the building. He cycled past the Grove cinema and over the wooden Nelson bridge towards the school. It was almost dark as he approached the shed.

'Help me,' croaked a voice.

Clarence flashed his large handlamp at the shed door. 'Is that you Turner?' he asked curtly.

'Yes,' croaked a voice.

'What on earth are you playing at, man?'

'I'm locked in, yer fool, wadya think,' came the reply.

'Don't be impertinent to me my good man,' snapped Clarence. 'And look at this door, look at the state of it, it's school property you know.'

'Are you going to talk all night or get me out?' roared the caretaker.

'Where's the key, the lock's closed?' he said angrily.

'It wasn't, somebody dun it,' wailed the caretaker.

'Where's the key you fool?' bawled Clarence.

'I've got it,' came the reply.

'Push it under the door you dunderhead,' shouted Clarence.

'Don't you call me names,' yelled the caretaker.

'The key, idiot, the key,' bawled Clarence.

As the key appeared under the door, the headmaster came striding up. He was usually a placid man but now he was angry.

'What is all this pandemonium?' he demanded.

Clarence unlocked the door. 'Our fool of a caretaker managed to get himself locked in,' he said, opening the door.

'Don't you call me a fool, you windbag,' snorted the caretaker as he emerged.

'That's quite enough of that Turner,' snapped Mr Alton.

'Look at this door.' Even in the dark it was noticeable.

'I'll repair it headmaster,' said the caretaker, now in better control of himself.

'See you do. How did this happen?' demanded Mr Alton.

'That Crabb boy, I bet he did it,' replied the caretaker.

'Did you see him?' asked Clarence.

'No,' replied the caretaker truculently.

'Then you cannot be sure. I dismissed him and saw him running off home,' said Clarence.

'If that is the case it was not him,' said Mr Alton, who at heart was a very fair man.

'You cannot blame Crabb for everything, Turner.'

'No, headmaster,' mumbled the caretaker.

'I'll get back to my duties,' said Clarence importantly. 'You are not locked out of your house by any chance, Turner?' he said sarcastically.

'No,' growled the caretaker.

Having parted company with the headmaster and caretaker Clarence cycled towards the seafront. He had arranged to meet Mildred Pullen at the corner of Grimstone

Gardens adjacent to her house. It was now dark and a blackout was strictly enforced.

It was just after 10 when he and Mildred went into the beach hut, and this time he took the precaution of taking his bicycle in with them. He pulled the door closed and turned on his lamp. Unbeknown to him, his movements had been under surveillance. Even though it was dark, Johnny Crabb had followed him from school with the stealth of a commando.

The beach hut, Johnny had noticed during a daytime observation with Jimmy King, had a hasp and staple on the door but no padlock. It was a substantial fitment for a well-made door. Johnny had found an old padlock and key, a massive thing about the size of a saucer which, though rusty, did work. Waiting a few minutes to allay any suspicion by Clarence and his companion, Johnny crept forward from his hiding place. He could hear movements inside the hut as he put the padlock on. The key was stiff but turned. Johnny crept a few feet away and picked up a half a brick, and then threw it in the air so that it would land on the roof.

In the silence with only the gentle lapping of the waves at low tide, when it landed on the roof it sounded like a thunderbolt.

He heard a scream and a yell, then he threw up larger boulders and the screams continued. The door of the hut rattled as Jimmy ran off.

He raced back to the Grove cinema. The programme had another ten minutes to run, the foyer was deserted and he went inside.

'I left my cap,' he said to the usherette.

'You can stay here and wait until its over,' she said severely, having had to tell him twice during the evening to be quiet.

Johnny stood next to the usherette, he made no comment which was unlike him but then she was his alibi.

Meanwhile, Clarence was getting desperate as he banged on the door in an effort to obtain some help, whilst Mildred Pullen was crying loudly.

'Will you shut up, you stupid bitch,' he snarled as he flashed his lamp around the hut. They were trapped, there was no window; it was like a box with a lid.

'Don't you speak to me like that, Clarence,' sobbed Mildred. Clarence ignored her and banged on the door. The noise at last attracted attention and the police were telephoned. The sergeant arrived to see a number of people outside the beach hut and he could hear shouts from inside.

'Is that you, Constable Bristol?' asked the sergeant.

'Yes it is,' replied Clarence.

'What are you doing in there for heaven's sake, man?'

'Helping Mrs Pullen to find her cat. Someone locked the door on us,' said Clarence.

'There is a massive padlock on it, have you got a key?'

'No, I have not,' snarled Clarence.

'Then we will have to get the fire brigade to get you out, they have got equipment to get this padlock off.'

With the help of the fire brigade Clarence and Mildred Pullen were at last released and greeted by the grinning sergeant and firemen who were all smiling.

'Did you find Mrs Pullen's pussy?' asked the sergeant.

Clarence, pushing his bicycle, almost knocked him over in his haste to be away.

'It's that Crabb boy,' he hissed shaking with rage. 'I'm going to get him,' he snarled.

'Now!' bawled the sergeant, grabbing at his own cycle.

Clarence pedalled furiously, whilst the sergeant desperately tried to keep up on his bicycle as they went in the direction of the Crabb cottage.

Such was his anger that he threw his cycle down on the shingle as he approached the little wooden gate of the cottage. Thump, thump, thump, Clarence banged the knocker on the front door of the cottage with some force.

Mrs Crabb, a worried look on her face, opened the door and peered into the dark outside.

'It's me, Mr Bristol Mrs Crabb. Where is your son?' he demanded.

'In bed of course,' replied Mrs Crabb, clasping her hands.

By this time the sergeant had arrived, breathing heavily.

'I want to see him,' he said pushing past her and running up the stairs.

Johnny could hear the noise and with his head under the bedclothes kept his eyes closed.

'Mr Bristol, you have no right,' said Mrs Crabb, following him upstairs, the sergeant following her.

Mrs Crabb turned on the bedroom light and Johnny blinked his eyes. 'Wot is it Mum?' he yawned.

The sergeant spoke, anger in his voice, as they left Johnny's bedroom and went downstairs.

'Now are you satisfied Bristol? I'm sorry about this Mrs Crabb, come Bristol, that is an order.'

As they slowly pedalled back to the police station the sergeant said, 'You realise Constable that Mrs Crabb could bring charges against you and I would have to substantiate them.'

Clarence Bristol grunted. He knew that the sergeant was right, but he was not going to admit it to someone he considered his intellectual inferior.

It would be all around the town tomorrow and he would be a laughing stock. His face burned in spite of the cool sea breeze. If it was not Crabb who was it? he pondered.

The thought nagged his brain and that night he pondered all possibilities in his mind.

The following morning the headmaster called Clarence into his office. His face was grim. 'You overstepped your authority last night Mr Bristol, and there could be serious repercussions I am informed.'

'I realise that, headmaster, and I regret it,' replied Clarence, his manner unusually contrite.

'From what I have been told it could well have been Crabb but you know well enough you have to prove it. That boy is as hard as nails and he will never admit to anything to either of us. I have already seen Crabb and he claimed he was at the cinema using a complimentary ticket given him by King.'

'Good heavens, King giving out complimentary tickets, whatever next,' said Clarence.

'Yes it makes one wonder just what the world is coming to,' said the headmaster in a tired voice. 'I have spoken to the manager of the Grove cinema who knows Crabb, which will not surprise you, and he states he was there when the last performance finished as there was a scuffle between him and another boy. Added to which he was told to keep quiet by the usherette during the evening. Again, I can believe that, which means if you were locked in that beach hut before ten it could not have been Crabb as the last performance finished at approximately ten-fifteen.'

Clarence nodded, 'Yes headmaster, so it would appear.'

'That will be all,' said the headmaster curtly.

The incident did not go any further as Mrs Crabb wisely did not lodge a complaint, though she did call on Mr Alton and point out that Canon Godwinson, the chairman of the school governors, had christened Johnny.

'Its a pity he did not drown him in the font,' said Clarence when Mr Alton had informed him of her visit.

'Perhaps our task would now be a little easier,' conceded the headmaster tiredly. 'But she did point out her husband is serving in the county regiment overseas and that Canon Godwinson is a chaplain to the regiment, so take heed Mr Bristol.'

'I take the point, headmaster,' nodded Clarence. 'As you say, evidence,' he added.

'Exactly, Mr Bristol,' the headmaster replied.

13

During the following days there was something of a hostile truce between Clarence Bristol and Johnny Crabb. At times the master seemed to deliberately ignore Johnny, and the cane saw much less use.

Daylight raids over Germany and other targets were becoming more frequent and if the planes returning flew low overhead the noise was such that the windows rattled and the teachers could not be heard. The low drone of their approach was noted by the boys and hands would go up in the classrooms.

One morning Ginger Baker was sent home by Mr Alton.

'What did you say, King?' snapped Clarence.

Jimmy reluctantly stood up before he replied, 'I said I bet his mum has had a telegram like my mum had and Potter's mum had,' said Jimmy sadly.

For once Clarence did not snap back at him as he said quietly, 'You could well be right lad.'

It was nearly play time and the drone was getting louder.

'The American planes are coming home sir, can we go out and wave to them sir?' pleaded Jimmy.

Clarence nodded and got off his counting house type chair. 'First row file out orderly to the playground and be quiet.'

It seemed all the classes were going out and the noise was becoming almost deafening. The sky now became filled with planes, squadron after squadron of bombers, the gaps in the squadrons were numerous and the planes were quite low. Some had pieces of their wings missing, others portions of their tails. The children waved and pointed at the sky, giving their own welcome to the brave airmen returning home.

One Sunday morning Johnny, armed with his bamboo fishing rod and a packet of sandwiches his mother had given him, called for Jimmy at the pub.

It was not yet opening time and Johnny went round the back and banged on the kitchen door.

Jimmy's great aunt Alice opened it and peered at him.

'Oh it's you, is it?' she said. Her iron grey hair was pinned up under a head scarf and she looked bleary eyed. 'Wait a minute,' she growled, closing the door.

Two minutes later Jimmy appeared carrying a bottle of Whites lemonade and a packet of crisps.

'Hi, Crabby,' he said as he slammed the door.

'Gordon Bennett,' they could hear his aunt say, 'he'll smash that door one day Ruby.'

'Come on, let's get off,' said Jimmy, grabbing at his bamboo cane that stood against the wall. He sensed storm clouds on the horizon.

Johnny hurried out of the yard after him and into Stade Street.

'Wot time you gotta be 'ome?' asked Johnny,

'Me dinner's at four o'clock,' replied Jimmy.

'Four!' replied Johnny in surprise.

'Pub don't shut till three,' explained Jimmy as they walked down Stade Street towards the canal.

'I don't feel 'ungry at four,' sniffed Jimmy. 'And if I don't eat it my aunt goes potty.' He put down his bottle of lemonade and spread out his arms and spoke in an affected voice. 'There I am slogging and slaving at the gas stove and this ungrateful boy will not eat his food.

Johnny started to laugh as Jimmy picked up his bottle of lemonade.

'Gets me into trouble it does, my mum goes on at me,' said Jimmy miserably.

'Does yer aunt slog and slave at the gas stove?' asked Johnny, looking at him curiously.

'Nar, she's in the larder 'alf the time,' replied Jimmy.

'Eh, why?' frowned Johnny.

'Cos the whisky is kept there, she keeps 'aving sips all day, 'eard my Uncle Frank say the other day. By rights she should be as pissed as a newt by two o'clock.'

'Is she?' queried Johnny.

'Dunno,' replied Jimmy, 'she don't look any different.'

'Hm,' nodded Johnny, 'maybe she's pissed all the time,' he said philosophically.

'Anyway, she don't like me,' continued Johnny emphatically.

'Nar, she don't, says you're a bad influence.'

Johnny stopped and turned and faced his friend. 'Why?' he demanded.

'Cos she says you swear,' replied Jimmy.

'I bloody don't,' replied Johnny hotly.

Jimmy shrugged his shoulders, 'That's what she said,' he replied.

'That's a bleeding liberty,' grumbled Johnny. 'I s'pose she blamed me for those cracks in your kitchen winder,' he said as they tramped down the road.

'Nope she didn't,' replied Jimmy. 'Blames the winder cleaner fer that.'

'Eh?' said Johnny in surprise.

"Yer, she don't like 'im since someone told 'er that he was in the Nelson pub saying her beer was flat.'

'Ha, ha, ha,' chortled Johnny, 'Not her bitter, after you give it a lift with 'orse shit.'

'Shut up about that, Crabby,' said Jimmy with a worried look.

'Does ole Keeler still 'ave his three pints of bitter?' asked Johnny, laughing.

'Nar, gorn orf it,' replied Jimmy, 'says its too acidy for

'is stomach, drinks bottles of Guinness now.'

'Not surprised,' sniffed Johnny.

'I brought me dinner,' he said, patting his canvas fishing bag, which was slung around his neck.

'My mum gave me a bag of crisps and I nicked a bottle of lemonade,' he said holding up the bottle of White's lemonade.

'We'll share,' said Johnny, taking his packet of sandwiches out of his bag and showing them to Jimmy.

'Alright,' agreed Jimmy.

By this time they were going past the side of the school where the caretaker's house was situated. Mr Turner was quietly hoeing his front garden on this peaceful Sunday morning.

'Look its ole Turnip,' said Johnny with a grin.

''Ere lets sing "O dear wot can the matter be," said Johnny, bursting into song.

The caretaker looked up as the boys started singing, his face now bright red and shaking his fist at them. 'You little bastards,' he bawled at them as they started to laugh and run off.

He was still shouting at them as they ran down to the canal and walked along the footpath.

'Let's fish by the Red Lion Bridge,' said Johnny walking ahead.

'Alright,' agreed Jimmy.

The Red Lion bridge was named after an adjacent public house and was the next bridge up the canal after the Nelson bridge. Both were popular fishing spots for the boys. Further up was the Romney Hythe and Dymchurch Light Railway bridge, near the school's allotments; not such a popular spot with the boys due to the amount of weed and barbed wire in the canal at that point. They sat on the parapet of the Red Lion bridge for about an hour without any success.

'It's too bleedin' windy 'ere,' complained Johnny as he pulled in his line.

'Yeh,' agreed Jimmy, 'let's go down past the Light Railway bridge, we got plenty of time.'

'Wot about this side of the light railway?' said Johnny.

'Nar, the soldiers in the huts by the canal told me to clear off the other day,' replied Jimmy.

'Alright, we'll go down ter Palmarsh, past the Light Railway bridge,' said Johnny.

Soon they were walking along a shady path that ran parallel to the canal until they left the environs of Hythe. Now on either side of the canal were fields. It was a warm dry day and they took a rest, lying in the grass with their hands under their heads looking up at the sky. Vapour trails were visible all over the sky and minute dots could be seen by the boys' sharp eyes.

'There's a dog fight goin' on up there,' said Johnny.

'Yeah looks like it don't it,' agreed Jimmy.

Lieutenant Claus Albrecht eased back the throttle of his Messerschmitt 109. The engine began to cough and black smoke began to emerge from the cowling. Quickly he glanced at his fuel gauge; the needle was almost on zero. His sharp eyes scanned the sky above and around him; he was alone as far as he could see.

Vapour trails criss-crossed the sky above him. Below he could see the English channel and coastline.

Yes, he was losing height and engine speed was dropping, no question of it. Getting back to base was now out of the question. It must have been his lucky day; by all the rules he should have gone down in flames, half his squadron had already done so but not before they had inflicted similar losses on their British counterparts.

The fuel gauge was now on zero, meaning he had ten

minutes flying left at most. He glanced below him, the thought of landing in the sea was not appealing. Perhaps he could make the French coast, he would try. But as he moved the controls something happened. The plane seemed to judder and shake, then flames burst from the engine cowling. He banked the plane towards the English coastline; it was now or now or never, he could explode at any moment. Unfastening his seatbelt he released the canopy and the air rushed past. Pulling himself up into the air, a push, and he was falling and the air howled in his ears.

For a moment he thought the parachute would not open. He had pulled on the cord, it must, then he felt a jerk around his chest and under his arms, it had opened thank God.

He heard a bang behind him then all was quiet and he was alone. Of his plane there was no sign, it had just disappeared.

It looked as if his war was over; would he receive a hostile reception, he wondered?

He looked down at the English coastline. At least he could speak the language, it seemed a lifetime ago since he had been teaching English at a high school in Bonn, but it was less than three years.

Now he was a fighter ace with nine kills to his credit. Perhaps it was an omen, the sequence nine, and his luck had run out.

He drifted towards the coast. Perhaps he would not get wet after all, he mused. There was a dryness in his throat and he suddenly felt hungry.

It was Sunday. No party in the mess for him tonight dammit. His thoughts turned to his wife Heidi and their two little girls, the apartment in Bonn and their cottage in the country. The last two years had been good for him, almost a bachelor again, with admiring glances at parties and willing partners it had been an extension of his carefree university days. Now it was to end. At least, he reflected, he was still alive, unlike many of the pilots with whom he did his flying training. The old faces were fewer, but were they old? He was old compared to most of them, some five to seven years in many instances. How would it all end, he asked himself? Like the Great War all over again, as far as fighter pilots were concerned, it seemed to be. It saddened him when he thought of his friends. Gunther dead, Lothar dead, Hermann missing, Manfreid missing presumed dead, the list became longer by the week and now he would be on it, part of the squadron's statistics.

Heidi, how would she take the news? Tears perhaps, he could not be sure after the scene over a mutual female friend on his last leave. No, she would take it as a stoic German National Socialist housewife and put the children first. Money would be no problem, her father was wealthy, a prosperous metal founder for whom the war had been a blessing in disguise. Not that Heidi needed her family money; she was a part-time nursing sister at a nearby military hospital and with his pay could manage very comfortably.

He looked down. The ground was fast approaching and it was still touch and go if he landed in the sea.

A gust of wind caught him, taking him inland. He could see fields and what seemed to be a river that appeared to run parallel to the sea.

The ground came rushing up. 'Mein Gott I'm going in the river after missing the sea!'

Before any more thoughts could go through his mind he hit the ground with a thud. It was a good landing, not because of any landing skill on his part but because he fell in a marshy field with long grass which cushioned his fall.

He struggled to his feet; the wet marsh seeping through

his flying gear precluded any sitting position. As he gathered up his parachute he was aware he was being observed by two boys, who stood still, each holding a long bamboo cane.

'England, ja?' he said with a grin.

'Blimey,' mumbled Johnny now only three paces from the man. 'A German, it's a German, Kingy,' he gasped.

The airman smiled, 'I am German,' he said in English without any trace of an accent.

'Yer won't shoot us, will yer?' said Johnny anxiously.

'Shoot you? Of course not,' smiled the airman. 'Now I must gather my parachute,' he said as he pulled the cords towards himself.

'Ain't it a smasher,' said Johnny running forward to assist. Soon both boys were pulling on the shrouds.

'It would make a smashing tent Crabby,' said Jimmy as they helped fold up the parachute.

'Yeah, do you want it mister?' asked Johnny.

Claus Albrecht hesitated, unsure what to say. He frowned.

'We'll swop it wiv yer,' said Jimmy. The German pilot frowned. He did not understand the meaning of the word 'swop', it was new to him.

'Swop? Swop, boys, what is that?' he asked.

'Exchange,' said Jimmy quickly.

'Ah, I understand. What for?' he grinned.

'I'll give yer a sandwich, Kingy 'ere has got some crisps and lemonade,' said Johnny hopefully.

The airman who was relieved to be both in one piece and out of the war, smiled and nodded.

'A swop it is,' he chuckled.

Soon they were sitting on the canal bank sharing their food with the German airman.

'What is your name?' asked the airman as he took the lemonade bottle from Jimmy.

'I'm Jimmy King, he's Johnny Crabb,' Jimmy replied.

'Jah!, and I am Claus Albrecht, call me Claus,' he said taking a long swig from the bottle. 'I used to be a schoolmaster before I became a pilot.'

'A what?' said the boys in almost unified horror.

'Ja, in Bonn I taught English.'

'A schoolmaster,' repeated Jimmy now holding his hand out for the bottle of lemonade.

'Are you fishing?' asked Claus as he looked at their discarded bamboos with the lines and floats attached to them.

'We was,' said Johnny.

'Where's your plane?' asked Jimmy.

'In the sea I should think,' grinned Claus. 'Where are your fathers?' he asked unexpectedly.

'Mine's in the army in India I think,' said Johnny.

Jimmy had bowed his head, he looked up his eyes misty, 'Mine's in the navy, my mum says his ships gorn down and they are all gorn, I don't believe her, he's coming home, he promised.' He turned to Johnny. 'He did, didn't he Crabby?' he said urgently.

'Yeah he did,' replied Johnny quickly.

'Then he will come home Jimmy,' said Claus quietly, 'a promise is a promise and from one's father that is a special promise Jimmy.' The airman looked away in embarrassment, now regretting he had asked the question.

Having consumed some of the food and drunk half the lemonade, Claus spoke again. 'I suppose I must find a policeman and surrender,' he said reluctantly, stretching his arms.

The station sergeant at Hythe police station put down his telephone. It had been a busy day for a Sunday and now a parachute was reported landing down on the marshes.

'Constable Bristol, would you join the Home Guard unit next door and go down to Palmarsh, a parachute has been seen to land near the canal, six Home Guards and a sergeant are going with you.'

'Yes, sergeant,' replied Clarence Bristol as he went out of the door of the police station.

The lorry whined as the Home Guard driver put it into third gear.

'It needs a decoke,' explained the driver to Clarence, who was sitting: next to him. The Home Guard sergeant sitting on the other side of Clarence was more succinct.

'It's bloody knackered George, that's why we've got it.'

The driver did not reply and the lorry coughed and struggled through the town until they were driving down the Dymchurch Road on their way to Palmarsh.

Leaving the built up area behind, the road was now four feet above the level of the land on the canal side, on the opposite seaward side it was the same level, being dunes and shingle. The lorry whined but kept going and as they went round a bend, the driver pointed.

'What's that?' On the footpath on the canal side of the road were three figures. One was a tall blond man in flying gear and next to him was a boy with what seemed a screwed up parachute on his head, and next to *him* was a boy holding two bamboo fishing canes.

'That's him, must be,' said the sergeant excitedly,

'Isn't that one of your boys constable?' he said, pointing at Jimmy.

Clarence Bristol leaned forward in his seat his mouth open.

'Oh my God, I don't believe it,' he paused and shook his head, 'I might have guessed King, and Crabb, no doubt, under that parachute, it's unbelievable,' he murmured.

The lorry wheezed to a halt and the Home Guard and Clarence climbed out.

'We were just taking Claus to the police station, Mr Bristol,' explained Jimmy.

Clarence nodded and said tersely to Johnny, 'Put the parachute into the back of the lorry Crabb.'

Johnny, whose head was now just visible, looked aghast.

'It's ours, sir,' he retorted.

'Yours? What are you talking about boy?' he snapped.

'Claus give it us, sir,' said Johnny standing his ground.

'Gave it to you?' Clarence frowned.

'Yes, sir,' Jimmy retorted, 'we swopped it for some of our sandwiches and lemonade.'

The German airman was grinning, as were the Home Guard. This seemed to antagonise Clarence, who stormed, 'I've never heard such nonsense,' he thundered, grabbing at the parachute.

Johnny Crabb however was not cowed. He gripped the parachute as Clarence pulled and suddenly let go. Clarence staggered backwards, clutching the parachute. Unfortunately he tripped and went backwards off the footpath and fell down the slope to the drainage ditch and landed in six inches of stagnant water with the parachute on top of him. The roar of laughter above him acted like a catapult on Clarence, he clambered up the embankment, pulling the parachute after him, and stood upright on the pavement.

'That was your fault, you horrible object,' he shouted as he lunged at Johnny, SMACK, his hand caught Johnny's ear, SMACK, it landed again.

'Leave the boy,' said the airman, stepping forward, ignoring the Home Guard rifles.

The German need not have worried. Johnny swung his right boot which though it did not have a full set of blakeys as they were unobtainable, nevertheless had one in the toe and it caught Clarence on the shin.

'Ow ow ow!' howled Clarence, 'you wretch, I'll cane you on Monday,' he gasped, clasping his shin.

Taking the attitude that he might as well be hung as a sheep as a lamb Johnny swung his boot again and his aim was true, for this time it was the other shin.

'Ow ow!' howled Clarence. The Home Guard and the German airman were now convulsed with laughter.

'It's my bleeding parachute,' shouted Johnny, grabbing it.

Clarence however didn't let go and the Home Guard sergeant still laughing, intervened.

'I'll take it, my lad,' he said.

'Why?' said Jimmy, grabbing at it, 'It's ours.'

'It's not, he is our prisoner,' said the Home Guard importantly.

'I surrender to them,' grinned Claus, pointing to Johnny and Jimmy.

'See!' glared Johnny.

'You keep out of this,' said the sergeant, turning to the German airman, his smile now gone.

'It's government property now, in the lorry all of you,' he said sternly.

Clarence glared at Johnny. 'I'll deal with you later boy,' he hissed, as he rubbed his sore shin.

'You 'it me first,' retorted Johnny, 'I'll tell my mum.'

'Can we 'ave a ride back?' asked Jimmy.

'No you cannot,' said the sergeant severely.

The boys watched as the parachute was put into the back of the lorry and the men climbed into it.

''E 'ad half my lemonade,' shouted Jimmy at the driver's cab, holding up his lemonade bottle. 'It's a bleedin' swizz, that's what it is,' moaned Johnny as the lorry engine started and the driver turned the lorry around. As the lorry passed them on its way back to Hythe, Johnny jerked up his hand and gave the sergeant and Clarence the V sign. The Home Guard were laughing and they heard Claus call to them from the back of the lorry, 'Goodbye, Johnny, goodbye Jimmy.'

'Bye, Claus,' they replied, returning his wave.

Claus Albrecht waved to the boys until the lorry picked up speed and the boys disappeared from view. He felt a little miserable, sorry that he had not been able to give the boys his parachute after accepting their food and lemonade, and sad for the boy whose father would not be returning home after the war. The fair haired boy with the corduroy lumber jacket had appealed to him, the aggressive look and eyes that filled with tears when he spoke of his father. For the first time he realised how children were affected by the war. Would his daughters miss him like that, he wondered. No, he doubted it, after all they were only five and six years old, but could he be sure of it he wondered?

As the lorry negotiated a bend, the boys carrying their bamboo canes with the fishing lines attached could no longer be seen by the German airman, it was if they had never existed.

At 4.30 Jimmy was having his dinner.

'What yer been doing?' asked a bleary-eyed Uncle Frank.

'We captured a German airman down at Palmarsh,' he answered.

Suddenly his mother's hand shot out and landed on his ear.

'Ow, what's that for?' demanded Jimmy.

'Telling lies again,' she hissed.

'Weren't a bleedin' lie,' protested Jimmy.

'Listen to his language, it's that Crabb boy,' said Aunt Alice with a sniff.

'He can go straight to bed after this, I'm fed up with him,' snapped Ruby King.

Jimmy did not reply but looked down at his plate; if only his dad would come home, he thought.

14

Perhaps it was the fact that the local newspaper photographer took a picture of Clarence with the captured German airman and gave an assurance that it would be in the local newspaper the following Wednesday that made Clarence overlook the little fracas that took place with Johnny Crabb the following Monday morning.

Not that this worried Johnny; his concern was the parachute that should have been his property.

When Clarence discussed the matter with Mr Alton, the headmaster was moved to say with a faint smile, 'It makes the adventures of Tom Sawyer seem rather tame does it not Mr Bristol?'

'Even Mark Twain in his wildest imagination could not dream up a pair like Crabb and King,' said Clarence, breathing hard.

'I think you may have a point,' murmured Mr Alton.

The story of Crabb's parachute had gone round the school by the time playtime began on Monday morning and Johnny was holding forth on the matter, surrounded by Georgie Cloke, Billy Collins and their pals.

'It's a bleedin' liberty,' he began, giving vent to his feelings. He then made it clear in no uncertain manner what he thought of Clarence and the local Home Guard. 'I swopped it for two sandwiches, 'alf Kingy's crisps and some lemonade.'

'He had 'alf the bottle,' said Jimmy quickly.

'It 'ud made a smashing tent,' said Johnny mournfully, 'and that silly sod of a Home Guard stuck 'is oar in too, that was our parachute, not 'is.'

Still complaining they went back into school and the uneasy truce that existed between Clarence and Johnny Crabb continued.

It was at this time that the raids on Germany were beginning to increase and in the playground at playtime and at dinnertime they would count the squadrons coming home, noting a gap in a formation here and another gap there.

'Look, Crabby, that formation has lost four,' said Jimmy one dinnertime as they gazed up in the sky.

'Yeah, musta been shot down,' said Johnny. 'That one over there 'as lost five.' He shaded his eyes as he counted the planes.

'Hope Chick is alright,' said Jimmy anxiously, 'he don't 'ave no mum or dad,' he added sadly.

'Yeah,' replied Johnny.

'Come from an orphanage,' said Jimmy quietly. 'Hope he's alright.'

Johnny did not reply as he was engrossed in his own thoughts.

'Fishin' after school?' asked Jimmy.

'Nah.' Johnny shook his head. 'Got ter help me mum, it's 'er wash day and I turn the mangle for her washin'.'

At that moment the school bell rang and they lined up in their classes. Then they were told to assemble in the school hall as the headmaster had something to say.

'Might be another free trip to the pictures,' said Terry Kelly.

'Could be,' agreed Johnny.

When they were all assembled in the hall the headmaster stood on the rostrum to address them. Terry's guess was however some way short of the mark.

'I've had a complaint from the manager of the Ritz cinema today,' he said sternly.

Hythe boasted two cinemas: the Grove, overlooking the

canal in the centre of the town and the Ritz at the far or Folkestone end of the town. The Ritz was the smarter of the two and the prices of admission were accordingly higher.

'He tells me that boys have been causing trouble by throwing conkers at the usherette and trying to trip up the lady with the tray of ice cream and soft drinks. I wonder at times if the school has the right motto.' The headmaster sighed and pointed to the two-foot high letters painted high up on the wall at the end of the assembly hall. 'Manners Maketh Man' it read.

Clarence rolled his eyes and Mrs Woollet passed a hand across her mouth, whilst Miss Darrowfield had to blow her nose.

'Crabb, do you know anything of this business?' snapped Mr Alton.

'No, sir,' replied Johnny, an innocent expression on his face.

'That surprises me, doesn't it you, Mr Bristol?'

'It does, headmaster. I find it hard to believe,' replied Clarence.

'When were you last there, Crabb?'

'Can't remember, sir, I was banned a long time ago,' replied Johnny.

'How wise of the manager and fortuitous for you this time Crabb,' said Mr Alton, compressing his thin lips.

'It wasn't my fault sir,' protested Johnny, 'that my ferrit got out of me pocket and escaped and that woman started screaming fer nuffin just 'cos it ran up her legs.'

'Be quiet, Crabb, I have no wish to hear of your entertainment problems; it is your own fault. King, what do you know of this?'

'Well, sir, it's as Crabby said, the ferrit was in his pocket and the woman hit it wiv 'er 'andbag and it bit 'er.'

'I am not concerned with that. Do you know anything of this latest episode?'

'No, sir, I was banned too,' replied Jimmy.

'And why were you banned?' asked Mr Alton, who immediately realised it had been unwise to ask.

'Well, sir, I lost my grass snake in there, I was on the front row and I think it went behind the curtain, sir, 'cos the curtain is green.'

'Good heavens, have you no sense? You do not take animals into the cinema,' said the headmaster tiredly.

'It don't say yer can't take ferrits and grass snakes in outside, sir,' protested Jimmy.

'It does not say you cannot take horses in, does it boy, but you do not, do you?'

'No sir, but yer couldn't, the doors are not wide enough and my grass snake is still in there 'cos the manager wouldn't let me look for it, he just banned me and I've got a complimentary sir it's a bleedin' liberty.'

'Be quiet boy, if you swear again I will cane you.' Mr Alton was going red in the face and Clarence was enjoying the exchanges, judging by the faint leer now appearing on his face.

'Kelly, what do you know of this?' snapped Mr Alton.

'Nothing, sir.'

'Have you been banned as well?'

'No, sir,' replied Terry, aghast.

'Cloke, do you know anything about it?'

'No, sir,' replied Georgie Cloke.

The headmaster soon realised he was wasting his time, so after a severe warning they were sent to their respective classes.

After school Johnny and Jimmy discussed the matter of going to the Ritz cinema.

'It was all Clokey's fault, trippin' up that ice-cream woman,' said Jimmy with a sniff.

'We got an ice cream each,' pointed out Johnny.

'Yeah but they'll watch the emergency exits now, it was daft, I'm not giving Clokey my complimentary ticket next week.'

'Why not? You can't use it,' said Johnny.

'Maybe, but if my aunt finds out that Clokey is letting us all in through the emergency exit she won't give it me again and the Grove one too, and there's a circus on the green next week. She's got a poster for that and I want that ticket,' said Jimmy with feeling.

''Ere,' said Johnny thoughtfully, 'is there an emergency exit in the big top?'

'I don't bloody know,' replied Jimmy well aware what Johnny was going to suggest next.

That evening his aunt duly gave him the circus ticket and Jimmy waited expectantly for the arrival of the Sir James Dilwall's International Circus.

The arrival of the circus was the subject of much discussion by Johnny Crabb and the rest of the lads at playtime. ''Ow much are the tickets?' asked Ginger Baker.

'Start at two shillings,' said Johnny. 'My mum says its too much, eight shillings for all of us.'

'You've got some money from yer firewood round,' said Jimmy.

'Yer an you've got a free bloody ticket,' retorted Johnny. 'I'm not goin wivout me sisters and that's that.'

'What about you, Kelly?'

'Dunno, me mum said she'll think about it,' he replied.

'Couldn't you make some wiv your printing outfit, Kingy?' said Johnny reflectively.

'No, I couldn't,' said Jimmy quickly.

'Well, there's only one thing for it, you'll 'ave ter lift the flap up at the back of the big top and let us in Kingy, as you've got a ticket,' said Johnny.

''Ave ter see,' said Jimmy thoughtfully.

Sir James Dilwall's International Circus duly arrived and their vehicles and trailers parked on the green adjacent to the school. The circus big top was erected on the green in front of the school and as Johnny Crabb, Terry Kelly and Jimmy King waited in the playground for the school bell they could see men assembling the poles for the big top.

It was a windy day and Jimmy looked up anxiously at the sky. 'Hope this wind packs up,' he muttered.

'Won't,' said Johnny emphatically. 'It's from the south-west and gettin' worse.'

Terry Kelly nodded. 'They'll never get that top up, it'll be blown away in this wind.'

'That'll be 'andy,' sniffed Johnny, 'then we can all get in.'

'They'll not 'ave a bloody circus without a big top and they're only here for a day,' said Jimmy, a choke in his voice.

The school bell began to ring and they lined up in their classes before going into school.

The morning dragged on and Jimmy kept turning to look out of the classroom overlooking the green.

'King, come out here, I've told you already to stop turning round,' snapped Clarence, who had taken his cane out of the cupboard. 'Hold out your hand, boy.' Thwack, thwack. 'Now the other one.' Thwack, thwack. Jimmy bit his lip and returned to his desk. He tried to write but he could not hold the pencil.

'They can't get that big top up, Kingy,' whispered Johnny.

'And it's only here for a day,' said Jimmy miserably.

'It's not much anyway. They've only one elephant and that can't stand up,' whispered Johnny.

'Why?' asked Jimmy, a frown on his face.

'It looks too bleedin' old,' replied Johnny with a grin.

'Crabb and King, if you talk again I will cane you both,' snapped Clarence, glaring at them.

The day progressed slowly, by mid-afternoon the wind had not abated and there was still no sign of the big top going up.

Johnny Crabb turned and looked out of the window. 'It's gettin' worse,' he said to Jimmy.

'Sod it,' muttered Jimmy.

'Crabb, King, come out here,' bawled Clarence, going to his cupboard and taking out the cane. 'I've told you both enough times to do your work. Hold out your hand Crabb.' Thwack, thwack, thwack, Clarence brought the cane down with all his force. 'Other hand Crabb!' snapped Clarence. Again the cane mercilessly fell on Johnny Crabb's grubby hand. 'Now you, King,' growled Clarence.

'But sir, I've already—' began Jimmy.

'Hold out your hand, boy,' Clarence glared at him.

Jimmy held out his already sore hand and when he returned to his desk he was fighting back the tears.

'You're not blubbing are you, Kingy?' whispered Johnny.

'No, I'm not,' sniffed Jimmy.

Jimmy sat with his hands under his arms as Clarence Bristol walked around the classroom. It was five minutes before dismissal and Jimmy still had most of his work to do.

'Why aren't you writing, King?' barked Clarence.

'I can't hold my pencil, sir,' replied Jimmy miserably.

'Then you will have to stay behind after school won't you?' came the sarcastic reply.

Jimmy got out of school at five. The circus vehicles were about to leave. Jimmy cast a glance in their direction but made no attempt to cross the green to see them. Instead he went home. He sat dejectedly in the kitchen, his hands still numb. His uncle Frank looked at him, a cigarette in his mouth had burned down almost to his lips.

'What's the matter with you?' he said, folding his newspaper.

'Got caned twice today and the circus is goin',' sniffed Jimmy.

'Got caned twice eh? S'pect you deserved it,' was his uncle's unsympathetic reply.

When he told his mother and then his aunt neither of them offered him any sympathy and after eating his tea in silence he left the pub and went to meet Johnny Crabb.

He found Johnny on the seafront at the end of Stade Street, gazing down the deserted promenade.

'Just seen ole Clarence on his bike,' said Johnny.

'In 'is special's uniform?' replied Jimmy.

'Yeah, the big nellie,' replied Johnny. 'Let's track 'im down, 'es gorn down towards Seabrook.'

'Yeah, let's,' agreed Jimmy.

They hurried along the Seabrook Road, passing the partially boarded up Imperial Hotel and its small golf course. Though there were mines on the beach, in places some had been removed now that the imminent threat of invasion had receded. Further on from the golf course was a small area of rough land or dunes which was also cleared of mines.

'There he is,' said Jimmy, pointing to a distant figure on a bicycle, pedalling towards them on the deserted promenade road.

'He's on his way back,' said Johnny, 'let's hide in the dunes.'

'Yeah, let's,' agreed Jimmy. They ran across the road to the dunes and scrub ground on the land side of the coast road. They kept well hidden in the dunes, watching Clarence pedalling slowly towards them, his progress hindered by the wind.

'Look, what's that Crabby?' Jimmy said, pointing to a bright object on the edge of the dunes a few yards from the road.

Johnny Crabb moved forward, much like the Indians he had seen in Western films, whilst Jimmy crept after him.

'Hold it,' said Johnny. 'It's one of those butterfly bombs,' he said. He backed away from the object and Jimmy did likewise. They took refuge behind a mound of sea grass and then Johnny spoke.

'Let's throw some stones at it from behind 'ere, it's safe enough.'

Jimmy did not need any encouragement and soon they had collected a pile of stones.

Clarence was about fifty yards away when they started to throw stones and some ten yards away when Johnny hit the bomb with a lump of brick.

Bang! The bomb exploded, throwing a cascade of sand into the air.

'Cor, that was a good bang,' said Johnny, shaking the sand out of his hair.

Jimmy was looking at the road; of Clarence Bristol and his bicycle there was no sign.

'Where's ole Bisto gorn?' he gasped.

Johnny started to run the few yards to the road, closely followed by Jimmy.

'Gawd,' muttered Johnny, looking up and down the deserted road, 'he's bloody gorn,' he gasped.

Jimmy looked up at the sky. 'D'yer think he's gorn up ter heaven?' he muttered.

'Wot, on 'is bike?' replied Johnny.

The answer was soon apparent. They could hear footsteps on the beach.

It blew 'im off the prom on ter the beach', said Johnny. 'Let's 'op it before he spots us.'

They ran back to the dunes and eventually Clarence appeared, trying to push his bicycle, which now had a buckled front wheel.

His jacket was torn and he was limping. There also appeared to be a lump on his forehead.

As they watched he pushed his cycle towards Twiss Road. From a prudent distance they began to follow as he made his weary way back to the police station.

When he was a short distance from the police station they ran and caught up with him.

'Please, sir,' began Johnny, 'I think we saw one of them butterfly bombs up near the seafront sir.'

Clarence Bristol, his hat askew, peered at Johnny Crabb, for once lost for words.

'Sir, your front wheel is buckled,' said Jimmy as he pointed to the battered bicycle.

Again he did not reply as he leaned the bicycle against the police station wall and staggered inside.

15

For the next three days Clarence Bristol did not attend school and his absence was not regretted by Johnny and his pals. Mr Alton took their class and Johnny Crabb and company thought that they were having a holiday.

On the third day just before first dinner bell the class was in something of a turmoil, Mr Alton having been called away. Johnny Crabb was firing pellets at girls on the front row. His prime target was Mavis Pullen who had moved there from the row in front of him.

He had just hit her with a pellet when the door opened and Mr Alton entered and shouted, 'Stop firing pellets, Crabb. Then he said in a quieter voice, 'Crabb.'

'Yes, sir,' said Johnny, standing up.

'Go and collect your sisters and take them home, your mother wishes to speak to you.'

'Yes, sir,' said Johnny in surprise. 'Now, sir?'

'Yes, immediately, lad,' said the headmaster in a kindly manner.

Johnny left the class and minutes later the first dinner bell rang.

'Wot d'yer think Crabby's gorn 'ome for?' asked Terry Kelly, who was sitting next to Jimmy.

'Dunno,' shrugged Jimmy.

'His dad might 'ave come 'ome on leave,' said Georgie Cloke.

Jimmy stopped eating, his appetite suddenly gone.

'Playing footer, Kingy?' asked Terry as they left the dining hall.

'Nar, I'm goin ter take some fish to Charlie the drayman,' he said running across the school playground.

The fish were in a bucket of water in one of the outhouses behind his great aunt's pub and as Jimmy was taking them out his Uncle Frank looked in the doorway.

'What have you got there?' he demanded, a slur in his voice.

'Some fish for Charlie the drayman's cat,' replied Jimmy.

Frank Summers peered at the five little roach and sniffed. 'Not very big are they?' There was a grin on his bloated purple coloured face.

Jimmy looked at him, the eternal cigarette in his mouth burnt down almost to nothing. His uncle did not believe in waste.

'No they ain't,' he admitted.

'I'll give yer a pound if yer catch me one over a foot long,' Frank Summers laughed deep in his throat, he did not throw his money about or make rash bets.

'Alright Uncle Frank, I'll catch one,' said Jimmy eagerly.

His uncle ambled off, still chuckling to himself as Jimmy wrapped his five little roach in newspaper.

Charlie the drayman was a man in his sixties, his dray with his horse Mabel were outside his cottage when Jimmy arrived.

'Hello, Mabel,' said Jimmy, patting her neck. Mabel however was not interested in him, she had her nosebag on and shook it at him in disdain.

Jimmy knocked at the green painted back door and Charlie opened it.

'Hello Jimmy,' smiled Charlie, 'come on in, son.'

Charlie and his wife did not have any children of their own but kept three cats.

'Got some fish for yer, Charlie,' said Jimmy as he put the package on the kitchen table.

'Hello Jimmy,' smiled Charlie's wife as she came into the kitchen. 'Brought some fish for my cats?'

'Yes Mrs Charlie, five roach,' replied Jimmy.

'Here's sixpence, Jimmy,' said Charlie, taking out a leather purse.

'Thank you,' said Jimmy putting it in his pocket. 'I lost a hook on one of those roach, bloody thing swallowed it and I busted the catgut getting it out.'

Charlie and his wife were now smiling broadly.

'Cost me four pence,' said Jimmy with feeling.

'Oh dear,' said Charlie's wife. 'Look Jimmy I've got something for you. She opened a cupboard and from a bag took out an orange. 'Here you are Jimmy,' she said, offering him the orange.

'Cor, fer me?' he beamed. Oranges were rarely seen in the shops and were something of a special treat.

'Yes, for you. My young brother in the Merchant Navy brought some home when he was last on leave.'

Jimmy held the large orange, then sniffed at it. 'It smells nice, I'll give a bit ter Crabby,' he said.

'How's your mum these days now that...' Charlie's wife paused. Charlie frowned and shook his head at his wife who immediately stopped talking.

Jimmy looked from one to the other. His mouth had screwed up, then he spoke, his eyes wide as he began. 'My dad's comin' 'ome, he promised and a promise is a promise.'

Charlie nodded. 'Of course he is son.'

'Even that German pilot said so, he said when a father makes a promise to his son it's special,' said Jimmy. So there.'

Charlie's wife wiped the corner of her eye on her apron.

'What German pilot Jimmy?' asked Charlie curiously.

'That one that came down at Palmarsh the other Sunday, it was in the local paper wiv ole Clarence's picture.'

'You spoke to him?' frowned Charlie in disbelief.

'Corse, he landed right where we were fishin', Crabby and me gave him sandwiches and crisps and lemonade for 'is parachute, but that ole bastard Clarence wouldn't let us 'ave it, bloody liberty I call it when it was ours.'

Charlie and his wife were endeavouring not to smile.

'It 'ud made a smashing tent but that 'ome guard sergeant said it was government property, it weren't it was Crabby's and mine, he drank 'alf my lemonade.'

'The German pilot did?'

'Yes Charlie, we were takin 'im to Palmarsh police station when we met Clarence and that big shit of a 'ome guard sergeant, he surrendered to us yer know not to Clarence and the 'ome guard,' said Jimmy frowning.

This was too much for Charlie and his wife, who doubled up with laughter, as Jimmy stood there, a perplexed look on his face, then he heard the school bell.

'Aw sod it, I'll be late,' he said opening the back door and hurrying out. 'Bye,' he shouted over his shoulder.

'Bye Jimmy,' chorused Charlie and his wife, both still laughing heartily.

'Oh! that boy is a caution,' said Charlie's wife, drying her eyes on her apron.

'Aye he is that,' agreed Charlie, 'he's sixpenny worth of entertainment. He won't accept the fact that his father will not be coming home,' his face was now serious as was his wife's. 'It's a shame, it means so much to him, I don't think his mother is too concerned from what I hear.'

'They could have let those boys keep that parachute, God knows the kids get little enough. Hilda Crabb works from dawn to dusk to keep her three clothed and fed.'

'That's a fact,' agreed Charlie.

'There isn't much justice in this world,' said Charlie's wife sadly.

After school Jimmy made his way to the Crabbs' cottage. Much as he had been tempted to eat the orange he had resisted and it was still bulging in his pocket.

It came as a surprise to Jimmy to find nobody in. After knocking at both the front and back door Jimmy left and made his way home. As he went down Windmill Street he saw one of the Cloke brothers.

'Seen Crabby?' he asked.

'Yer, down by the Nelson bridge,' replied Dave Cloke.

'Ta,' said Jimmy, starting to run. He called in at the pub to be told his tea would be another hour yet, so he took his fishing bamboo and hurried down Stade Street.

He could see Johnny Crabb hunched up over his fishing bamboo, sitting under the Nelson bridge. Jimmy ran down the canal bank to him.

'Hey Crabby, you've gotta bite,' he said as the float bobbed up and down.

Johnny Crabb ignored him. As he got nearer Jimmy could not believe his eyes. Johnny Crabb was crying, tears streaming down his face.

'Crabby!' he gasped, 'you're blubbing.'

'No I'm not, it's the wind, its cold 'ere,' he began, then he paused.

'Me dad's been killed,' he muttered miserably.

'Ah, Crabby,' Jimmy murmured, sitting down beside him.

'Me mum gotta a telegram this morning,' he sniffed.

'I called for yer at your 'ouse,' said Jimmy.

'Me mum's gorn to me gran's with the girls,' said Johnny.

'Mrs Charlie gave me an orange, I saved it so you could 'ave a bit,' said Jimmy, showing Johnny the large orange.

'Don't wan' it,' sniffed Johnny.

They sat in silence for a while looking at the water. 'You can 'ave my flare parachute for a week,' offered Jimmy.

'Don't wan' it for a week,' replied Johnny shortly.

Jimmy took the flare parachute from his pocket and put it in Johnny's hand.

'You can 'ave it, Crabby, I can find another one,' he said quietly.

Johnny Crabb's face lit up. 'Yer mean I can keep it?'

'Yeah, corse yer can,' replied Jimmy.

Johnny Crabb put the flare parachute into his pocket, 'I've always wanted one of them,' he smiled. ''Ere, I think I'll 'ave a bit of your orange after all.'

16

A few days later the boys were fishing in the canal just past the Red Lion bridge. Some soldiers were fishing further down the canal and one of them called to Jimmy.

'Wanna fish, son?'

Jimmy put down his bamboo and ran along the canal bank. Outside the temporary wooden buildings that the soldiers occupied was a large tin bath half filled with water. In it was a carp, the biggest Jimmy had ever seen; it was almost two feet long and its girth must have been some twenty inches, truly a monster.

'Cor what a whopper!' gasped Jimmy.

Behind him an army corporal began to laugh. 'Like it, son?' he asked.

'Cor yeah,' nodded Jimmy.

'Take it then,' said the corporal with a grin.

Jimmy needed no second invitation. He grabbed the dead fish by its tail and lifted it out of the tin bath.

'Cor thanks mister,' he said as he staggered back to Johnny Crabb with his fish.

'Bloody 'ell,' said Johnny when he saw it. 'Its the biggest carp I've ever seen, what yer goin' ter do with it?'

'My Uncle Frank said he would give me a quid if I caught one over a foot long,' said Jimmy.

'Yeah but you didn't catch it,' pointed out Johnny with a sudden burst of honesty.

'No, but he don't bloody know that,' said Jimmy, exasperation in his voice. 'I'll give yer 'alf if you 'elp carry it 'ome.'

'Ten bob,' said Johnny, who had never had as much money at one time in all his life.

'Yer on,' he said, picking up the fish.

They hurried home as fast as carrying the large fish would allow them and eventually arrived at the lounge side of the North Star Inn. It was 2.20 p.m. and as it was Saturday Uncle Frank and Great Aunt Alice could be relied on to be sitting on bar stools in the lounge bar with their elbows on the bar.

Both were there as usual, drinking their whiskies and ginger ale. His mother was behind the bar and there were only two other customers on the far side of the lounge.

'Hello, what have you got there?' asked Uncle Frank as he blinked blearily at Jimmy and Johnny as they came close to him carrying the fish.

'There, Uncle Frank,' said Jimmy, holding up the fish proudly with both hands. 'It's longer than a foot, what about my quid?'

'Quid?' frowned Uncle Frank, who had just received some unpleasant news at the local bookmaker. 'I didn't say a quid, tanner more like.'

'You did say a pound?' said Jimmy, his voice rising.

'I'll give yer sixpence that's all,' replied Uncle Frank as he dug into his pocket and pulled out a sixpence.

Jimmy took it, his face glum, 'but you said a quid,' he protested.

'I didn't.' Uncle Frank's face was now the shade of pickled cabbage and his voice was rising.

'You did, you mouldy ole shit,' howled Jimmy.

'What!' roared Uncle Frank and Aunt Alice in unison. They both struck out at Jimmy, not a wise thing to do when only half sober and sitting on bar stools. Jimmy jumped back with the agility of a mongoose as they toppled off the bar stools.

CRASH, with a yell they both hit the lounge floor which near the bar was not carpeted.

Jimmy and Johnny beat a hasty retreat out of the bar and into the back yard where Jimmy left the fish and his bamboo rod.

'Can I come 'ome with you, Crabby? I'll give yer 'alf the sixpence,' said Jimmy in a worried tone.

'Yeah come on,' said Johnny as they ran out into the road.

Jimmy felt at home in the Crabbs' neat little cottage. It was built on the shingle at the edge of the beach and there was not a plant in what passed for their garden.

Mrs Crabb was a thin little woman always doing something and looking permanently harassed and worried. The family were fisher folk, her father having been the lifeboat coxon for some years, and her brother was still fishing when on leave from the navy.

Johnny's father had worked for the council before he was called up and his family also had connections with local fishing, which accounted for the fact that fish figured largely in their diet.

'You can stay to tea, Jimmy, if you like. It's only fish,' said Mrs Crabb kindly.

'Yes please, Mrs Crabb, I like fish,' replied Jimmy eagerly.

Jimmy sat between Johnny's sisters, Jeannie and Violet. Unused to young company, having no brothers and sisters, Jimmy seemed in a different world, the cottage with its spliced ropes, and ships in bottles fascinated him.

The roof was corrugated and well covered in pitch. You could even smell it in the cottage. It was so homely Jimmy did not want to leave; he could have stayed there forever.

The cottage did not have electricity and at 9 o'clock Mrs Crabb lit an oil lamp, looking at Jimmy as she did so.

'Don't you think you should go home now Jimmy?' she smiled.

'Do I 'ave to, Mrs Crabb?' replied Jimmy miserably.

'They'll be wondering where you have got to,' said Mrs Crabb.

'Don't want ter go 'ome,' pouted Jimmy.

'But your mum, dear,' said Mrs Crabb patiently.

'She don't want me, I'm a nuisance, she said so,' he muttered.

'But you will have to go home Jimmy,' she smiled sympathetically. 'You can come again can't you?'

Jimmy nodded, close to tears, and at that moment there was a knock on the front door.

'See who that is Johnny,' said Mrs Crabb, tidying her hair.

It was Jimmy's mother and she was keeping her temper with some difficulty. Without a word of thanks to Mrs Crabb who she considered her social inferior she grabbed Jimmy by the arm and pulled him down the garden path.

'I don't wanna go home with you,' he wailed.

Ruby King glared, her face red with anger and exertion. 'The trouble you've caused, Aunt Alice has sprained her ankle and Uncle Frank's got a broken collar bone,' she hissed.

'Wasn't my fault,' protested Jimmy.

Mrs Crabb watched the exchange without a word, then with a shrug of her thin shoulders closed her cottage door.

17

Some days later Johnny and Jimmy were playing outside the Crabbs' cottage. There was a faint drone of aircraft and the boys looked up at the sky.

Whilst they were doing so Mrs Crabb came out of the cottage with two pieces of bread pudding on a plate. 'Here you are, boys,' she smiled, 'eat it while it's warm.'

'Thank you, Mrs Crabb,' beamed Jimmy, taking a piece of her delicious bread pudding.

'How's your aunt, Jimmy, after her accident?' she asked, a faint smile playing around her mouth.

'Alright,' replied Jimmy, his mouth full of bread pudding. 'She spends most of her day sitting in the larder now, don't slog and slave at the gas stove no more. I get sent down to the British restaurant in the Red Lion Square now with a tray to get dinners from there. My Uncle Frank keeps saying it's cold by the time I get back, he's an ungrateful ole shit Mrs Crabb,' said Jimmy with feeling.

Hilda Crabb was doing her best not to laugh outright as she said sympathetically, her hand to her mouth, 'It's almost half a mile from your aunt's pub to the British restaurant.'

Jimmy nodded as he replied miserably, 'I know Mrs Crabb. Last week my uncle said I'd forgotten the gravy and I 'ad ter go back again and they're bleedin' rotten dinners anyway.'

Mrs Crabb now had both hands to her mouth and she turned to go indoors. Once inside she started to laugh as she had not done for ages. Holding her sides she laughed away all the tensions caused by her recent bereavement as she thought of Jimmy King and his British restaurant dinners.

'Cor, look at them,' said Johnny, pointing to the sky. Squadron after squadron of heavy bombers were coming in from the sea and the noise became so great that the boys began to shout in order to make themselves heard.

'Must 'ave been a big raid last night,' said Jimmy.

'Yeah, Mr Darkie says the Americans raid by day and the RAF by night,' said Johnny.

'Look, that formation's got three missing and that one's got five,' said Johnny pointing at the sky.

'I wonder if Chick's up there,' said Jimmy as he started to wave at the squadrons.

'He can't bloody see yer from up there,' said Johnny.

'Come on, let's go down the beach, the lifeboat's out.'

Jimmy trampled after Johnny down the shingle. They kept within the ropes on the section of the beach that had been cleared of mines and watched the lifeboat in the distance, making its way home.

Albert Darkie, the coastguard, was standing near the small wooden jetty when he spotted them.

'Keep clear you boys, we don't want you in the way,' he said brusquely.

'Why, Mr Darkie?' asked Johnny.

'Because they've been out to try and rescue the crew of a crashed American bomber,' he replied tersely.

They watched in silence as the lifeboat approached the jetty. Quickly it was tied up and four of the crew lifted out an object in a tarpaulin. They walked slowly up the beach followed by the coastguard and the boys.

On the promenade was an ambulance. The lifeboatmen gently put down their load, and Johnny and Jimmy stood next to them watching curiously.

The flap of the tarpaulin fell open to reveal the figure

of an American in flying gear. Jimmy stepped forward, the figure seemed asleep there was not a mark on his face.

'Is he dead, mister?' asked Jimmy quietly.

'That's right, son,' replied the lifeboatman.

Tears began to roll down Jimmy's cheeks as he clutched at Johnny's arm.

'It's Chick, Crabby, it's Chick,' he sobbed.

One of the lifeboatmen turned to Albert Darkie. 'Look at that kid from the pub Bert, crying his heart out and he's a little terror most of the time.'

Albert Darkie nodded. 'Aye, kids are funny ain't they?'

The ambulance men brought a stretcher and put the body of Chick on it, as Jimmy, still crying, was trying to wipe his eyes on the sleeve of his lumberjacket. He sniffed and turned to Johnny who had not spoken.

'I'm not crying, Crabby, it's the wind,' he said, rubbing his eyes.

'Nar,' said Johnny sympathetically. 'It's a cold wind, 'ere you 'ave it,' he took the flare parachute from his pocket and pushed it into Jimmy's hand. 'Go on, I don't want it any more,' he said quietly.

18

James King sat up on the wooden seat. He could feel tears on his cheeks as he looked at the spot on the promenade where Chick's body had lain.

'Hello, Jim,' said a voice. His wife and family had returned.

'Hi, dad,' said his son with a grin.

'Are you alright, Jim?' asked his wife peering anxiously at him. 'You look as if you have been crying.'

'No, love,' he replied, wiping his eyes with a handkerchief. 'It's the wind, it blows quite fresh here. Shall we find a café and have a coffee?'

'Good idea, Dad,' said his daughter-in-law.

He stood up and they walked slowly to their car. As they got into the car he looked at the promenade for the last time.

'Didn't you tell me of a particular friend you had as a boy who lived near here, named Fish or Fisher?' said his wife.

'Crabb,' smiled Jim as he started the car. 'I'll drive past their cottage in a moment. That's it, it's still there,' he pointed at the Crabbs' cottage as he drove slowly past, making a mental note of all the changes.

The lifeboat station had gone, as had the fishing boats.

'There it is,' said Jim, pointing to a pretty little cottage with tubs of flowers around it. The shingle that surrounded it was now a paved patio and a sailing dinghy was outside the back door. A small detached garage had been built and electricity appeared to have been laid on, yet it looked much the same.

'Isn't it a pretty little place?' said his wife as he stopped the car and the memories came flooding back.

'Didn't you say he went away, Jim?'

'Aye I did. Johnny went to Australia in the fifties, so I was told some years ago by a lad named Cloke who we had both known. He also told me that he had a successful lumber business in Queensland and that his mother and one of his sisters had gone out to join him.'

'It's strange, isn't it Jim, that you both have successful businesses yet neither of you had anything to start with,' remarked his wife as he switched on the ignition.

Jim shrugged. 'Perhaps that's the reason,' he replied quietly. 'We had nothing, asked for nothing and expected nothing, perhaps that's the trouble with the kids today, they expect too much. I'd like to see Johnny again, we'll have a holiday in Australia one day and try to look him up.'

'That would be nice Jim,' beamed his wife. 'When?' she asked enthusiastically.

There was no reply as he was now deep in his thoughts.

'Looks like a holiday place now, Dad,' said his son.

'Expect it is, more's the pity,' murmured Jim as he depressed the clutch and looked in the driving mirror.

He drove down the road past his old school. There were no children about as it was holiday time, it had not changed, it looked just as he remembered it.

He was almost sure he could hear children singing, 'All things bright and beautiful all creatures great and small.' He drove over the Nelson bridge, a lump in his throat, no longer the rattle of boards as the car passed over it. He turned left to go to Red Lion Square and out of Hythe.

His family had not spoken; they could tell he was upset.

'I shall never come back,' he said at last. 'I should never have come back this time, I'm a stranger,' he muttered, tears in his eyes.

'They say you should never go back, Jim,' said his wife as she affectionately squeezed his arm.

'No,' he murmured in agreement.